Somewhere in the Shallow Sea

A Novel of Suspense!

Ron + Marie - I hope you enjoy the read :)

Denniswriter2015@gmail.com

Dennis Macaraeg

Somewhere
in the
Shallow Sea
by
Dennis Macaraeg

dennismacaraeg.com

ISBN-10: 1517437954
ISBN-13: 978-1517437954

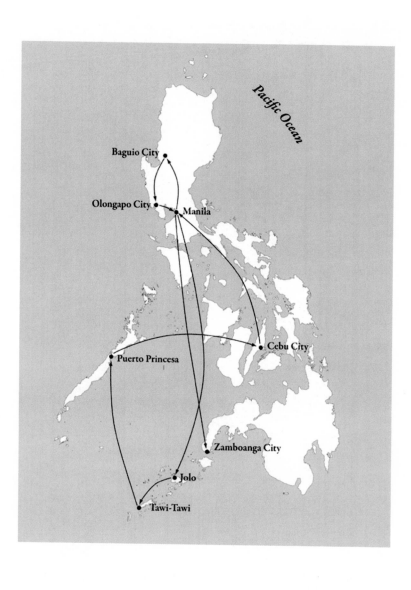

One

ON THE GLASS-LIKE SURFACE of the Pacific Ocean, the sun floating high in the sky reflected a silver sheen through the office window of Danilo "Danny" Maglaya's laboratory. The thirty-year-old marine biologist placed the handset back on the cradle, feeling troubled. It was the third time he had called the crew members of the *Desert Sea* via satellite phone in the last ten hours, but oddly, his calls went straight to the universal sound of voicemail. He knew that sometimes the weather conditions can affect global communications but those were only temporary. Worried that something had gone wrong, he hurriedly got up from his seat and as he was heading to the door to report the anomaly to his supervisor, he stopped in his tracks when he saw his company president, Jeff Smith, and an unknown man in a dark suit standing at the door. Jeff had never visited his office—not once in his two years of employment as a research scientist at SDM Biosciences. The combination of

Jeff, accompanied by a person he had never seen, sent alarms off in Danny's head, and he instantly thought that the grant for his research had run dry and his project would be shut down. He had feared this day arriving but it was the nature of business in the highly competitive world of marine biotechnology.

"Danny," Jeff said, his serious face directed at him.

"I was just on my way out to…"

"You might have been wondering why you haven't been receiving data from the *Desert Sea*."

"Yeah…this is highly unusual. Have there been issues with the ship's onboard communications gear?"

"The ship had been in total radio silence. Why don't I let FBI Special Agent McAllister give you the details?"

McAllister took a big step forward and said, "About four hours ago, we received a report from the captain stating that it was boarded by armed men in the southern part of the Philippines."

"How could that happen?" Danny faltered, looking straight at Agent McAllister. "Doesn't the Philippine Coast Guard heavily patrol the Sulu Sea? And aren't the U.S. Navy warships in the area conducting exercises?"

"These thugs drive speedboats. They can slip in and out without being detected," added McAllister with firmness in his voice.

Danny shifted his gaze at the ocean he had spent half his life exploring—where he found solace through roaming its reef and atolls. His knees weakened from the shocking news he just heard. He placed his hands on his desk trying not to lose his balance.

"According to the captain's initial report, a group of armed men on a fast-moving skiff approached and demanded to board the vessel," Jeff said.

"Did the crew try to defend themselves? Or shoot those bastards with flares at least?"

"They used water cannons but when the armed men started shooting, the captain ordered the crew to stop. Fearing someone in the ship might get shot, they had no choice but to let them climb onboard," Jeff added.

"Are those people still on the ship? Why don't you call in for some military action and send the Navy SEALs to surround it?" Danny responded, his voice cracking. "Don't let anyone get off."

"It's not that easy. The incident happened within Philippine waters and their government prohibits foreign interventions with domestic issues. Besides, the armed men were on the ship for less than half an hour and have already left," Jeff added.

"Can you please call the captain and order the ship to Honolulu?"

"It's on the way back to San Diego as we speak," Jeff said in a monotone voice. "We're already a step ahead in trying to resolve the crisis."

"I'm sorry to inform you but Blake Mason was taken," McAllister said with a straight face.

Danny couldn't believe his ears. Just a month ago he

was having a drink with Blake. He could still picture his unruly head of dark yellow hair, parted on the side, his long bangs covering half of his forehead. His slightly plump face hid behind the thinnest of beards. The thought of his best friend in the hands of money-seeking criminals was surreal.

"Was he kidnapped?"

"As of right now, we are treating this incident as a hostage situation," McAllister said.

"Why was Blake taken? Research scientists aren't rich."

"The agency is in contact with the Philippine authorities to figure that out," McAllister answered.

"How much do they want?" Danny asked, scared of the figure McAllister would blurt out.

"The group is demanding the Rx-18 compound as ransom," Jeff interrupted.

"The Cube? Only a few people even know it exists!" Danny exclaimed. "Why do they want my invention?" Bewilderment was palpable in Danny's face.

"We really don't know but the Philippine military are aware of the incident and already mobilizing their Scout Rangers to rescue him," McAllister said.

"What are we going to do while Blake languishes on some forsaken island?"

"Wait for further instructions," Jeff said. "That's all we can do for now."

"From who?" Danny said, frustration echoing in his voice.

"From the hostage negotiators as soon as contact is established."

AS SOON AS JEFF SMITH and Agent McAllister left his office, Danny stared at the Manila Galleon he kept on his desk. He had always been fascinated with Spanish trading ships and the year-round sailing voyages they made across the Pacific from Asia to the Americas during the Spanish colonial period. He couldn't just sit on the sidelines, waiting for the Philippine government officials in charge and hoping that their rescue efforts would be fast and decisive. Negotiations might drag on for months just like they had with previous hostage crises. Blake was probably suffering every minute he was held captive and would likely be killed if his abductors became frustrated with the slow progress of the negotiations. Danny felt he had no choice but to take care of business himself and bring the Cube to the kidnappers. But locating Blake's captors was not going to be easy. He couldn't guarantee that the American or Philippine governments would share their intelligence on Blake's abductors. And he especially needed the tactics they planned to implement for his rescue effort. Danny realized he might never see his best friend again if he put his blind trust in some government bureaucrat.

Danny knew he had to do something to save Blake even if doing so would potentially cause his own demise. He thought of that one fateful night in San Diego that forever brought their friendship into the heights of considering each other as brothers...

On a beautiful August night in downtown San Diego, Danny and Blake were walking on the street without a care in the world. They had just finished having dinner with friends. The sky was clear and the streets were filled with lovers holding hands. As they were rounding the corner, the saucy sound of a saxophone and the rhythmic beats of drums floating out of a jazz bar caught Danny's attention. Since the night was still young, he suggested to continue their celebration by listening to some live music. The line outside the club was long but no one was in a hurry to get home anytime soon. While waiting to get in, the commotion from a nearby boutique caught their attention. The high-pitched sound of the store alarm was going off, and a woman from the store came out shouting "Thief!" at a man in ski mask running out the front door. Two squad cars arrived. Weapons drawn, the police officers ordered the thief to drop his gun, but instead of complying, he became agitated and rushed at Danny. He was unprepared when the gunman grabbed him by the waist, pointed a Glock to his head, and ordered him to go with him. Danny tried to push him away, but the masked man smashed him in the back of the head with the gun.

Blake, not thinking of his own safety, jumped the masked man and pried his arm away from Danny. Then he heard the pistol pop and felt a searing pain cut through his shoulder. As Danny was falling, he saw the masked man on the ground as the police wrestled him and tried to cuff him. Turning paler with each passing second, Blake came to his aid immediately. He felt Blake's hand pressing over his shoulder where bright red blood was oozing. He could hear Blake shouting something at him but could not understand a word. He promised to the gods listening that he'd do anything to repay Blake's selflessness if he survived his ordeal. After what seemed to be a century, Danny finally heard the ambulance's siren wailing in the distance and then suddenly lost consciousness.

If Blake was willing to take a bullet for him in order to save his life, the least Danny could do was the same for him.

CONFUSED ON WHAT TO DO NEXT, Danny left his office to clear his mind and headed towards the edge of the cliff near his office building. There were tourists on the beach taking selfies and enjoying the crisp weather. Though the ocean wind stroking his face had a calming effect, it couldn't cleanse the sour guilt of passively letting the events take their unpredictable course. His thoughts turned to Blake, scared and lonely on some tiny island just beyond the horizon some 7,000 miles away. His mind raced with the million reasons why anyone would want the compound they had discovered together in their makeshift lab during the final years of their Ph.D. program in oceanography.

With Blake working on their company project about

the complex fish migration patterns on the research vessel in the southern part of the Philippines, Danny wondered if there was any connection to the Rx-18 compound.

Danny was desperate and knew there was only one person to call—Melchor Rodriguez, a biology professor who had been assisting Blake with his research. As he made the long-distance call, he hoped that Rodriguez would answer immediately. It seemed like an eternity as the sound of an overseas ring droned on and on until finally...

"Hello?"

"Professor Rodriguez, it's Danny. I'm calling from the States." He was relieved that Professor Rodriguez had picked up right away.

"I'm glad you called. I'm so pissed with what's happened to Blake."

Danny could sense blame in his voice's low tone.

"I thought the research vessel's operations were kept secret for security reasons?"

"That's true. I wasn't even told where we would drop anchor. It happened so quickly. All of a sudden, we saw a speedboat approach and then six armed men started shooting and demanded to board. Our captain tried to start the engine to get us the hell out of there but they were just too fast," Rodriguez said with apprehension in his voice.

Expecting the worst, Danny asked, "Was anyone hurt?"

"No, thank goodness. They only took Blake."

"I'm glad you and the crew are safe."

"How much is the group demanding?"

"They want the Cube," Danny responded.

"Isn't that the Rx-18 compound you two have been working on since college?"

"Yes, that's right. It's nothing but a supercharged food and I don't understand how they knew about it and want it so badly."

"I'm worried sick for Blake's safety. The radical group who took him call themselves 'Kulog ng Timog,' led by the crazed leader they call Commander Berto. They were responsible for beheading a British man a year ago because the ransom they demanded wasn't met."

"Why would those thugs want a scientific experiment?" Danny said, stroking his forehead to calm his nerves.

"It does not matter if this is about science or money. All I care about is getting Blake back alive and well. Can you come to Manila and bring the compound right away?"

"But how are we going to meet with the kidnappers?" Danny asked.

"As they were taking Blake, the group's leader gave me his go-between's contact number since I was translating for him. I had a feeling he knew who I was. No one knows I have it but I was instructed to send text messages only and to not pass the number on to the authorities or Blake would be harmed."

Danny paused for a moment. He knew that he had to take the Rx-18 compound and fly across the ocean to

Manila immediately if he wanted Blake freed by his captors.

"There is a flight leaving LAX tonight. I'll bring the Cube with me," Danny replied.

"That's great."

"Where can I meet you?" Danny asked.

"Get a taxi as soon as you land and tell the driver to take you straight to the university where I'm teaching."

Two

Danny's thoughts returned to his outbound flight 18 years ago when he was just twelve years old and his family was immigrating to America. It felt like a lifetime ago. His family had ultimately settled in San Diego. It hadn't been an easy adjustment but he had found comfort and inspiration in science. After graduating from high school, he majored in biology in college and then went on to graduate school. He had always known he would eventually visit the land he was born in but couldn't have imagined he'd be returning on a mission to save his best friend from getting killed by a group of kidnappers.

Manila. The city had been named after a flower and nicknamed the Pearl of the Orient. He still found it hard to imagine that for more than 300 years, the Spanish colonized the Philippines. Then, after the Spaniards left, the Americans took over spreading their own brand of colonialism. Just as the United States was about to return control of the islands to its native sons, the Japanese invaded in 1941. For almost four years, the Philippines was under the harsh control of the Empire of Japan. No wonder the Filipinos were wary of foreign intervention— even the kind that might be construed as benign help with no strings attached. The country now took pride in dealing with its own problems. It was a matter of showing the world that the Philippines could handle its own domestic issues. Danny knew this attitude made logical sense, but it wasn't going to make finding Blake any easier. Getting involved—and bringing the Cube—was the key to securing his friend's release and ending Blake's nightmare.

The chaotic and claustrophobic scene at the airport was intimidating, especially for someone who hadn't traveled to an Asian country in a long time. Though he spent his childhood in the streets of Manila, Danny now felt like a stranger in the Philippines. He spotted the lines of passengers standing next to their corrugated *balikbayan* boxes usually filled with chocolate candy, soap and Spam. Returning Filipinos with their balikbayan tourist boxes snaked around the open floor space as everyone waited for the customs agents to clear them, moving at a snail's pace. Danny noticed the Overseas Filipino Worker customs line. These hard-working men and women were commonly known as "OFW" and most had just returned from parts of Europe, Asia, and the Middle East. Most stood guarding their precious possessions bought after years of toil and time away from family and friends.

A customs official approached in a neatly-pressed uniform, asking if he had brought anything illegal into the country. Danny took a breath trying to calm his racing heart. If he didn't get the Cube into the country all hope of rescuing Blake would be lost.

"Just some personal items and clay," he said, casually pointing to the Rx-18 compound in vacuum-sealed plastic containers, neatly arranged in the rollaway bag.

The customs official took Danny's passport and compared his face to the photo inside. After a cursory look, he handed the passport back and smiled.

"Welcome back to the Philippines. *Mabuhay.*"

Danny tried to hide his relief as he slung his knapsack over his shoulder, grabbed the Cube's bag, and quickly exited through the airport's wide doors. Manila's hot and humid air welcomed him immediately. It kissed his face as if it was an old friend he had not seen in a long time. Beads of sweat began to form on the back of his neck, slowly rolling all the way down the groove of his spine. He wiped a layer of perspiration off his forehead and, summoning all his courage, walked out into the draining Philippine sun.

AS HE CRANED HIS NECK looking for a taxi, Danny noticed a man in blue jeans and a T-shirt looking straight at him with strange intensity. A cell phone in his hand. Something about the man was troubling. Disturbed by the thought that someone might be following him,

Danny pretended to not see the stranger and searched the immediate area for a quick exit. He spotted an OFW wearing a beige jacket with a black messenger bag hanging off his shoulder and pushing an overloaded baggage cart. He quickly stepped next to the OFW and casually followed him. Cars and vans clogged the airport's entrance as they waited for passengers exiting through the front door. Standing at six feet—taller than most Filipino men— Danny tried to blend in with the rest of the passengers waiting for their rides. He worried that he could be easily picked out in the crowd. With a quick backwards glance, he saw that the strange man was indeed following him, ever so slowly. Could there be others in the vicinity that might nab him? Who was this man and what did he know about the Cube or Blake's kidnapping? He continued to pretend that he didn't have a care in the world and wasn't aware of the man's presence. The last thing he wanted to do was create a scene. Without further delay, he stepped off the curb and onto the street of waiting taxis.

Danny climbed into the passenger seat of the first cab he saw and placed the Cube on his lap.

"Can you please take me to this place?" he asked, showing him Professor Rodriguez's business card with the university's logo.

"Okay, boss," the driver responded as he stepped on the gas pedal.

Danny looked behind him and saw the mysterious man standing at the curb texting a message on his phone, watching his taxi speed away.

The traffic along Roxas Boulevard was worse than he remembered, flooded with *Jeepneys*—Jeeps with elongated chassis and shiny chrome bumpers that serve as the most popular form of public transportation in the country. The box-shaped Jeepneys, with painted pictures of coconut trees swaying in the wind and portraits of beautiful, long-haired women on the side as part of their design, inched slowly on the street.

A young man walked by selling newspapers, holding a box filled with an assortment of gums and cigarettes. The headline read, "*American Military Bases to Return to the Philippines.*" His taxi driver held up two fingers and the street vendor handed him two loose cigarettes. The cab soon became unbearably hot. He couldn't tell what was hotter: the sun's heat beating down from above or the simmering warmth radiating from the asphalt road. Danny lowered his window hoping that the fresh air would provide some relief, but the city's muggy air drifted inside, contaminated with nauseating diesel engine smoke. He rolled the window back up.

Danny spotted the statue of Dr. José Rizal, the Philippines' national hero whose writings sparked the revolution against the Spanish colonizers in the late 1800s. The monument showed Rizal proudly flanked by statues of other revolutionaries from that time. The National Flag of the Philippines lined the promenade with its signature deep blue over scarlet red, with a white triangle at the hoist, a golden yellow sun and three stars. Two soldiers stood guard with rifles on their shoulders.

The cab driver seemed to sense Danny's anxiety, turned the radio on. The radio announcer was wailing about a senator caught with a 21-year-old college student in a leaked sex video. Danny could never understand how there could be thousands of hungry beggars roaming the streets and no one cared, yet an old man having sex with a young woman was newsworthy. The next story centered on exposing a public official who owned several lavish mansions yet had an "official salary" equivalent to only $1,000 a month. The driver switched to a different station. Now it was the voice of a folk singer crooning about an ungrateful son who left his family to pursue his dreams abroad only to return to find one of his parents had died.

"What's with the traffic?" Danny asked, peering out in the distance. "Are we ever going to move?"

"Too many cars in narrow streets and no one is following the traffic rules. Look at that Jeepney loading passengers in a no-loading zone. This traffic is as slow as a Quiapo Church procession, boss," the driver said, scratching his head as his face contorted into a look of frustration. "Would it be alright if we take side streets? It's a longer route but we'll be moving."

On the sidewalks, commuters tried desperately to flag down overcrowded Jeepneys. In the middle of the street, the traffic police halfheartedly tried to get the traffic moving, but the drivers just seemed to ignore them.

With the taxis, Jeepneys and buses driving up and down the avenues in an endless cycle of picking up and dropping off passengers, and with the motorcycles squeezing through every open space, it would take hours to arrive at his destination.

"I guess so," said Danny.

STILL RATTLED BY THE mysterious man at the airport, the oppressive Manila heat, and never-ending traffic jams, Danny had never been more relieved to exit the cab. Gathering his bag—and most importantly, the Cube—Danny entered the university grounds.

The students with their carefree expressions, knapsacks dangling down their backs, aimlessly meandered around the campus grounds oblivious to the real-world chaos just beyond the shelter of the university. He remembered his own carefree college days when his problems were purely academic and easily solved on the classroom's whiteboard or with the aid of his laptop. He missed those days. Life had seemed less complicated when his most pressing demand had been simply showing up to an English literature, biology or humanities class.

Danny soon found his way to the biology building and walked the length of the corridor leading to Professor Rodriguez's office. He dodged the students exiting their classrooms as they clutched their notebooks in a hurry to get to their next class.

A FEW MINUTES LATER, an amiable man with a thin, neatly-combed moustache and thinning black hair parted in the middle, arrived.

"Danny, I'm so glad you're here," Professor Rodriguez said, hugging him.

"How long has it been, Professor?" Danny replied as he stood back to look straight at a face that he hadn't seen in years.

"Please…just call me Melchor. No need to be formal."

"Sure."

"It's been four years since I last visited California. But come here, let's go into my office so we can talk privately."

When Danny entered the office, he noticed the salt-water aquarium in the corner right away. Butterfly fish and Angelfish glided over the artificial reef. He sat on the chair while Professor Rodriguez moved the stacks of papers and folders cluttering his desk.

"Never-ending term papers to check," Melchor commented.

"I have just as much paperwork waiting at my office when I return," Danny replied, trying to lighten up the mood.

Melchor walked towards the aquarium and dropped fish food in the tank. The fish hurried to the disintegrating flakes as they sank deeper in the water, like it was their last meal.

"This group is notorious for kidnapping Westerners and holding them for ransom. Usually they require a wire transfer, but this time the group's leader is demanding not only money but also the compound you've invented," Melchor said.

"I only brought the Cube with me," Danny replied, realizing the scope of the daunting task ahead of them.

"Don't worry about the money. Someone from the States is delivering it and due to arrive any moment."

"How do we meet the leader and these terrorists?"

"I have just texted their go-between and told him that the Cube and the money have just arrived."

"Who are these kidnappers?" Danny asked.

"At this point all I know is that the group's leader calls himself 'Commander Berto.'" He is well-known with locals in Southern Mindanao and had been terrorizing everything from Zamboanga City to Basilan and the Jolo Islands for many years. Many of the local people believe that he has an *anting-anting*—an amulet that makes him bulletproof."

"I can't thank you enough for helping me and sticking your neck out to get Blake back," Danny said.

"How could I not help? Blake has done so much for me and I would do anything to get him back. He was the one who guided me when I was new to the world of academia and helped me get my papers published. In a way, I became a professor because of him and I owe him my livelihood. You know us Filipinos...we have what's called '*utang ng loob.*' It simply means a debt of honor and that's what I owe Blake. In many ways, I am indebted to him. I want to repay this debt any way I can, especially in his hour of need. If I don't do everything in my power to get him back, and something bad happens, I just couldn't bear the consequences."

In a country where the concept of "*hiya*," or shame, was the last thing anyone wanted hanging over his or her head, Danny knew exactly how Melchor felt. If Melchor didn't step up to help save Blake he would lose face among his colleagues.

"I almost forgot that most unique Filipino attribute," Danny said.

"Doing something for Blake would give me a sense of '*amor propio*,' or self-respect."

DANNY UNZIPPED HIS CARRY-ON and checked the Rx-18 compound. He poked around the vacuum seal with his fingers and was relieved to find that the special plastic wrap hadn't punctured. He was about to close the zipper on the rollaway when he heard an all-too-familiar voice.

"Professor Rodriguez?"

Suddenly, Danny couldn't move his legs. His heart started to quiver. He recognized the low-pitched rasp coming from the woman speaking through the door. He hadn't heard that voice in more than three years. How could he forget her sweet tone when it had never really left the deepest chambers of his heart? He had truly loved her and yet he had spent so many long hours researching the

Rx-18 compound that he had unconsciously neglected her. Despite their love, they had slowly drifted apart. He was shocked to see her here, in the Philippines and in Melchor's office after so many years.

"Helen Glass? Is that you?" Melchor asked.

Danny found himself lost in Helen's blue-grey eyes. Her silky, light brown hair was still styled just as he remembered, curls flowing to the bottom of her shoulders. Helen moved closer to him as if making sure that Danny was really the man standing a few inches from her. The top of her head reached just above his nose. She wore a cream-colored blouse and skin-tight, black denim jeans that tapered down her thighs, highlighting the curve of her hips.

"Danny, what are you doing here? It's been a long time," Helen asked with a puzzled look on her face.

She stared into Danny's dark brown eyes and felt a mix of shock and regret, as she looked into the same eyes she had fallen in love with so many years ago. Danny still maintained his surfer physique with tight abs and muscles in his arms that resembled waves curling on the sandy beach.

"I'm here for Blake," Danny replied.

"You have the money the kidnappers are demanding? I thought I was supposed to bring it."

"I didn't come here with the money," Danny replied.

He was happy to see her again but at the same time resentful for their informal breakup many years back.

"Those animals who took Blake wanted money. What are you here for?" Helen replied, her voice elevating.

"What about you? How did you end up getting involved in this mess?"

Melchor stepped in between the couple attempting to clear up the confusion arising between them and said, "From what I observe, you two seem know each other."

Excited to see each other again after many years of absence, and at the same time worried for each other's safety, Danny and Helen didn't pay any attention to Melchor.

"Helen, meeting with the kidnappers is too dangerous for you. I think it might do you good to go back home," Danny begged.

"I don't think it would be less dangerous for you just because you've got a black belt in Arnis. Do you think waving a couple of fighting sticks will scare these men? These thugs carry AK-47s. They'll eat you for breakfast just like they'll have me for dessert. I've got the cash to get Blake back. Why are you here, exactly?"

"They're also asking for the Rx-18 compound," Danny replied, wishing she would board the next plane back to the United States.

Helen paused, not grasping what she had just been told.

"The compound you've been working on for five years? Why would they want that?" Her face showed a look of confusion.

"I'm planning to ask their leader, Commander Berto, as

soon as I meet him," Danny said.

"Well, without the money, the kidnappers will not release Blake. And that's why I brought it with me."

"You brought a million dollars with you?" Melchor asked.

"Are you crazy? It's not safe carrying that amount of money around here!" Danny yelled. "What if you get robbed? That's a huge amount of money to be carrying around."

"Well, I'm not just going to sit praying like a nun in a convent and hope everything magically turns out okay. I have to do something."

"You brought the whole amount with you?" Danny asked in disbelief.

"No. I just brought a hundred grand. The remaining $900,000 was deposited in a bank, and I will make a wire transfer once Blake is released to us," Helen replied.

Melchor tried to diffuse the growing tension in the room that was ready to bust the ceiling wide open.

"I don't think this is the time to debate who is or isn't going to help rescue Blake. You are both right— Commander Berto is demanding the money and the compound. I think it would be wise if you just cooperate with each other."

Danny realized that the only way to get Blake back to San Diego unharmed and to end his nightmare was to cooperate with Helen. He swallowed his pride, retreated and tried to calm down.

"What's the plan, then?" Danny asked, turning to Melchor.

"Blake is being held on the island of Jolo in the southern part of Mindanao. We'll fly there via a chartered flight that takes off in just over an hour. Once we land, we'll meet with a contact to take us to Commander Berto's camp. We will give him the Cube, make the wire transfer, and leave with Blake," Melchor said.

"How do we know this isn't a trick? Once he gets what he wants, what's to stop him from killing us all in the end? How can we be sure that we all walk away unharmed?" Helen asked.

"We don't know," Melchor replied. "And for all I know, he could order his men to execute us on our way back."

His bluntness had a layer of truth in it. Danny realized that he was going straight into the lion's den without a feasible exit plan.

"So we're all going on a suicide mission?" Helen asked.

"I've heard a lot about him. Commander Berto is ruthless, but for an evil man he has a word of honor. His business is kidnapping for ransom and the last thing he needs is the reputation that he kills his hostages and negotiators after he is paid. If that happens, no one will ever pay his ransom again. Believe me, dead hostages and negotiators are not good for business," Melchor said.

"Helen, please…for your safety, why don't you just give me the money and access to your bank account. Stay in a nice hotel and once we locate Commander Berto and

Blake, I will make the transfer and bring him back to you," Danny pleaded.

"Even if I wanted to, I couldn't. Our uncle, who issued the money, sent this as insurance," Helen said, holding up a flat, square device. "Before the money can be transferred, Blake and I must both place our thumbs on this scanner. The money will be released only after our biometrics are authenticated."

AT THE DOMESTIC SIDE of the Manila airport, their private, six-seater, twin-engine aircraft was fueled and waiting on the tarmac when they arrived. The pilot, wearing a white shirt and not looking a day older than Danny, stood by the plane's open door with a serious look on his face. Helen and Melchor climbed into the cabin. Danny followed and secured the rollaway luggage containing the Cube in the back of the plane. After fastening their seatbelts, they taxied to the main runway.

Danny stared at the side of Helen's face as she sat across the aisle, clutching the bag containing the ransom money. Just then, she turned toward him. He thought of trying to make small talk and asking how she'd been in the past three years in order to thaw the wall of ice between them but he quickly looked away—it was not the time to try to mend issues from their past.

As the airplane took off, Danny noticed the runway shimmering in the heat, creating a black liquid mirage. He wondered if going to Mindanao and attempting to rescue his friend was nothing but a false illusion that would result in a major snafu.

Danny looked at the empty seat next to Melchor. He hoped that come nightfall, Blake would be occupying it and that they'd all be safely back in Manila.

Three

FROM A FEW THOUSAND FEET up in the air, Danny felt intimidated by the island of Jolo. His pulse quickened at the thought of going straight to the Kulog ng Timog's main stronghold. Except for the main city center, the entire island was covered with a thick canopy of green trees. It was no wonder bandits like Commander Berto picked the island as a hideout. There were plenty of places to hide that would make it difficult for the authorities to find the Kulog ng Timog deep in the forest. Danny and Helen climbed down the airplane steps without exchanging a word. As he glimpsed at the menacing mountain in the far distance, he imagined Blake's bound hands and his thirst and hunger.

The small airport looked like a war zone. There was a heavy military presence. Armored personnel carriers and soldiers lying prone behind sandbags with M60 machine guns were positioned by the entrance. As he exited the airport with Helen and Melchor, Danny felt as if the soldiers were ready to shoot anyone perceived as the slightest threat.

Not wanting to attract attention from the Philippine Marines, they hurriedly walked away from the airport's fringes and into the busy street. For Danny, it was overwhelming to see the unfamiliar sight of men wearing skullcaps alongside women in long-sleeved blouses and black headscarves with baskets of fruits and vegetables hanging on their arms.

Seeing an empty Jeepney parked by the curb, Melchor approached the driver slouched on his seat.

"Can we hire you for the entire day?" Melchor asked, waving a thousand pesos in cash.

The driver pocketed the money, told them to get in and quickly shifted into first gear. Melchor jumped in the front seat while Danny and Helen followed and sat on the long, bench-style seats in the back.

The streets were clogged with pedestrians walking along the road. Children brazenly crossed the streets without care for their safety. The driver honked to warn them but they just ignored him. Avoiding an accident, the driver turned the steering wheel away from the crossing children and slammed on the brakes. The vehicle swerved to the right. Helen's knee brushed Danny's thigh. Their eyes met at their sudden unexpected contact. His heart raced.

Danny clung to the handlebars attached to the roof to keep from being thrown from side to side. He peeked outside to orient himself and saw the dome of a mosque with tall minarets pointing up at the cloudless sky, tucked behind wooden houses with rusty, corrugated roofs.

He wondered why out of all the things in the world, Commander Berto wanted the Rx-18 compound and how could anyone possibly know its existence. If another scientist was aware of it, it would be very easy to reverse engineer the compound's properties and reinvent it to a viable material. But what for? They were not doing anything out of the ordinary and several companies in the biotechnology field already had ongoing research for the same fish food technology. Danny and Blake had been working on developing the compound for four years and had tried mixing different chemicals and natural fish substitutes to make it work but their creation had yet to yield good results.

Danny and Blake wanted to create a compound like the Cube to save the world's fish population. The theory behind their invention was simple but profound. The compound would attract small fish, which in turn would attract bigger fish to follow, and thus be led to the protected waters that several countries had already agreed to create. Their goal was to save hundreds, if not thousands, of fish species from commercial overfishing.

DANNY HAD ONLY BEEN on the island of Jolo

less than an hour and he was already full of dread and despair. His only thoughts were for Blake's condition. Had a rope been tied around his waist so that he couldn't stray away, as if he were a farm animal? Danny wiped the sweat dripping on his forehead. *Mindanao.* The island's name itself evoked mystery and fear. He wondered how a place featured on travel magazine covers, surrounded by fine sand, picturesque coconut trees and clear waters could also be infested with rebels and outlaws.

THEY STOPPED ON THE SIDE of the road next to an open field.

"I think we are here," Melchor said as he checked the coordinates on his handheld GPS.

Danny grabbed the rollaway and climbed down the Jeepney's rear.

"We need to walk across the open field and go to the *nipa* hut. The guide will meet us there and then take us to Commander Berto's camp," Melchor said, reaching inside the bag for his 9mm pistol, a pair of small binoculars, and a two-way handheld radio.

"Do you have to bring that?" Helen asked.

"This is Mindanao. We're on our own and we need to protect ourselves from anyone trying to kill us," Melchor replied.

From where they stood, they could see several huts standing in the open field.

"Which hut do we need to go to?" Danny asked.

Melchor looked through his binoculars and surveyed the area. "The one with a white T-shirt flapping on the pole. It's about a half hour's walk."

THE NIPA HUT'S ROOF was made of dried brown straw and the walls were constructed with a lattice of split bamboos. Melchor approached the bamboo pole on the hut's side, took the white piece of cloth down and replaced it with a red scarf.

"I just sent a signal for our guide to come and get us. Why don't you two get inside to stay away from the hot sun and cool off? I'll wait here for our guide to fetch us."

Danny and Helen sat on the floor made from bamboos slats. They both found the wind blowing through the open windows refreshing. He unzipped his backpack and took out two energy bars.

"I think you might need one. We don't know how long this ordeal is going to last."

"Thank you," Helen replied.

She leaned on the wall and tore the wrapper open. As she slowly chewed, she began to reminisce about the first time she met Danny more than five years ago.

It was a summer night at a rented cottage on a beach in San Diego when Helen noticed Danny standing with Blake and several other friends, bottles of beer in their hands. There were at least two dozen people at the after-college-graduation get-together. As she mingled with the rest of the women in the party, she noticed Danny kept stealing glances at her.

Helen was curious about the tall, shirtless man with the even tan and with the big smile. From across the front yard, they had watched each other, both wondering how to get closer. Finally, Blake introduced them. At first, Danny tried to just give her a quick nod but Helen offered her hand. Though their handshake was light and fast—the kind where only fingers touch—their gaze was heavy and it was difficult for their eyes to peel away. She was sizzling with a hunger that she had never experienced with any man she'd encountered before —her deep attraction to him was almost primordial in nature.

The group spent the following day cooking, eating, drinking homemade sangria and lying on the beach. That night, while everyone was outside sitting around the bonfire half drunk, Helen noticed Danny stealing another peek at her. She knew that Danny wanted her and she wanted him, too. She crafted a plan to get him away from the group so they could be alone. While everyone was busy discussing whether grad school was worth the time and money, she got up, made eye contact with him, picked up the dirty glasses, and walked back into the empty cottage. A few minutes later, while standing next to a bookshelf with a book in her hand, Danny approached her. He asked Helen what she was reading. She turned it over and showed him the cover. By chance, she had picked one of his favorite books. Danny turned the pages and showed her his favorite passage.

Inches away from each other, the attraction that had been simmering since they had met the day before finally boiled over into a steamy passion. As if the stars above had already predetermined their next move, Danny and Helen kissed in the dimly lit living room.

DANNY HAD ALWAYS THOUGHT about the day when he would see Helen again. In his mind, they would meet at some unexpected party. She would be standing across the room and he would walk up to her and say hello. After talking awkwardly for a few minutes, the temperature in the room would immediately drop to an arctic level. They would run out of things to say and would part ways knowing that both of them had moved on with their lives and had nothing in common anymore.

He knew it would probably be better to leave their past in the confines of his memory, never to be revisited again. But, as he watched her sitting silently just a few feet away, he knew that his love—a love that had been simmering in his heart for years—was real and he would be stupid to let her slip through his hands once more.

"I didn't mean to raise my voice earlier. I was just surprised when you suddenly showed up," Danny said, looking directly at her.

"Forget about it. Both of us were a bit high strung from all the excitement. Besides, I yelled at you, too. I thought you were here for no reason. I'm sorry, too," Helen replied with a slight smile.

"Everything is happening so fast and we're both on edge."

"Sure is," Helen replied, taking a sip from her water bottle.

"It's been almost three years since I've seen you. What have you been up to?" Danny asked.

"I went back to school to earn my Masters of Arts in Education. I've been teaching in an elementary school in the Boston area for a couple of years."

"I wished I was there for you on your graduation day. I'm sorry, but I didn't know."

Helen crumpled the wrapper. "I didn't really tell most of my friends either. Just my immediate family attended."

"Seriously, I would have gone if I'd known."

"You and Blake have been working on the Rx-18 compound for almost five years now. Did you ever get any results? It's puzzling to hear that someone like Commander Berto, who doesn't know anything about it, let alone care for scientific research, would want to have your invention."

"That's what's been baffling me ever since Jeff told me that the Cube was one of the conditions for his release."

"Someone within your close circle who knows about the Rx-18 compound must be behind this kidnapping. There has to be more to this."

"How did you get involved in this mess?"

"Your boss called Blake's parents and told them what had happened. But the U.S. government officials told him that negotiating with terrorists, even if the company was willing to pay the ransom, isn't recommended. He was worried that the whole thing might end up in disaster so he hinted to Blake's parents that if they could come up with the money, something could be done. Blake's parents called me and told me what had happened and asked if I could deliver the money. I agreed so they passed on Jeff's contact number. Jeff told me to leave right away and to contact Melchor," Helen said.

WHILE DANNY TRIED to unravel her story, he heard a knock on the wall.

"Our pickup is here!" Melchor shouted through the window. "We need to go now."

Danny and Helen exited the nipa hut. They saw their guide standing next to Melchor, an older man wearing a wide-brimmed straw hat.

"Are you sure about him?" Danny asked.

"Not really. That's why I brought my 9mm with me, remember?"

"How would a single handgun even with a full magazine defend us from the AK-47s and M-14s those kidnappers have?" Helen interjected.

"Look. We don't know if this man will take us straight to Hades to meet Lucifer himself. We have no choice but to go with him. If you have doubts and think we shouldn't go with him, then maybe it's better to turn back now and let the authorities deal with the negotiations. Like I said earlier, Commander Berto wanted to meet with us because he wants to make the exchange now and get his money. What do you want to do, Danny?" Melchor asked.

Though he recognized that their situation was getting sketchier by the minute, Danny didn't see that they had any other choice.

"Let's get it done so we can all fly back to Manila with Blake by midnight," Danny replied, turning to Helen for approval.

DANNY, HELEN AND MELCHOR silently followed the guide. There was a sense of calm as they walked quietly across the field. Birds flew recklessly from the bushes. Cotton clumps of clouds floated over the mountains. Winds blew in from the ocean, ruffling the knee-high grass on the ground. They soon came across a small village with six wooden houses. Kids were playing a game of tag and adults were tending to a plot with tomatoes, onions and cabbage next to their houses. As they passed by, the residents momentarily stopped what they were doing with curious looks on their faces.

AFTER A FEW MILES OF HARD WALKING, they finally reached a shallow creek somewhere deep in the forest. The guide instructed them to stay behind while he fetched Commander Berto's men.

Weary but relieved to take a break from the long trek, they sat on the ground in the shade and waited for the guide to come back.

"You two sounded like an old married couple when you were arguing earlier," Melchor commented. "Is there something that I'm supposed to know?"

"Our paths have crossed," Danny answered, trying to downplay his past relationship with her.

"Are you sure it's just that?"

"We were once sort of engaged," Helen added as she clarified Danny's response.

"I'm glad that you two are involved in Blake's rescue," Melchor said. "Hopefully, things will go smoothly and we'll be off this island soon."

Danny lay on the ground, his hands behind his head, looking up at the coconut tree above as the sunrays flickered in between the rustling leaves.

"How are we going to make a wire transfer while we're in the middle of the jungle?" Helen asked.

"These guys have satellite phones and a setup capable of handling the transfer," Melchor replied. "They know what to do and all we have to do is follow instructions."

DANNY SAW A RIFLE'S MUZZLE pointed at him. His eyes traced the weapon and saw that it was an AK-47, held by a man in camouflage with a black bandana wrapped around his head. He quickly sat up and saw six more camouflaged men armed with rifles standing next to Helen and Melchor. It was one thing to search for the devil himself, and another to actually find him. Four of the men had black ski masks, but the other two didn't bother to conceal their faces. Danny felt a knot form in his stomach. He turned to Helen who had fear written all over her face. The men were more menacing in person than he thought. If someone had told Danny that one day he'd be staring directly at the faces of the pseudo-rebels notorious for kidnapping foreigners for money on a hot April day, he would have dismissed the notion as absurd. But here he was, inches away from the men who had taken Blake by force with their AK-47 and rocket launchers.

"I'm Commander Berto's right-hand man. Call me Vincent for now. My real name doesn't concern you. Yeah, just like the movie character."

"Do you have the money and the stuff we need?" said one of the unmasked men, a gold filling on his front tooth.

"Where's Blake?" Danny asked.

"He's not with us," Vincent replied. "We need to take you to a small island near Tawi-Tawi. A boat is waiting for us on the beach to take us there."

Danny thought about the absurdity of the man's arrogance for thinking he was some sort of Hollywood character and wearing American-made blue jeans. His group was known for publicly pronouncing their hatred for anything the West had to offer, and yet still enjoying the products it produces.

"Here's the money you want," Helen said, showing him the contents of her bag.

Vincent picked up a bundle of $100 bills, bent them

and ran his thumb on the edge of the stack. He grinned at the sight of the money and threw the stack back in the bag.

"The rest is in the bank. We will transfer the money as soon as we get Blake back," Helen said.

"Here's the compound you're asking for," Danny said, showing Vincent the contents of his carry-on suitcase.

"You just have to be patient. Your friend is getting our best island hospitality and has the best group of guys guarding him," Vincent replied sarcastically.

"We came here to give you what you want and to leave with Blake," Danny said.

"Commander Berto wanted to test your science experiment to see if it's working at all. What if you're just giving me a lump of shit?"

Going with the men to yet another island to rendezvous with Blake wasn't part of the plan but neither Danny, Helen nor Melchor dared to protest. Commander Berto and his men were holding all the cards and there wasn't anything they could do.

Just as Vincent was about to walk toward where he needed to take the group, a whistling sound came roaring across the sky. A bright flash burst through the ground with yellowish tendrils. Then, a deafening bang followed, disturbing the quiet afternoon. Milliseconds later, a puff of hot air slapped Danny's face and the overpowering smell of sulfur filled his nasal passages. Fearing for Helen's safety, he buried her face in his chest and dropped to the ground. Soil and pebbles rained on his back. The thunderous explosion muffled his hearing. All he could hear was the muted sound of weapons discharging from behind the trees.

"We need to get out of here!" Melchor shouted.

Danny grabbed Helen's hand while trying to avoid the bullets wheezing over their heads. Trying not to get shot in the crossfire, he led Helen as they ran and ducked toward the direction they had arrived at earlier. Melchor quickly followed.

"What's going on?" Danny yelled as soon as they were safely tucked behind a clump of tall grass.

"I don't know but I don't like it!" Melchor shouted through the mayhem.

"I think the Army Scout Rangers are here for an ambush," Danny said.

In response, Vincent threw several canisters of smoke bombs toward the trees where the shooting was coming from. Billowing red smoke engulfed the surroundings and the visibility dropped to zero. Through a tiny break in the smoke screen, Danny saw Vincent and his men running toward the other side of the creek and away from the hail of bullets the soldiers were raining down on them.

As if clouds had swallowed the entire forest, it was difficult to see in any direction. Careful not to get caught in friendly fire, the soldiers stopped shooting.

Helen shouted, "They can help us!"

"No!" Melchor fired back, "They will detain us for questioning and stop us from getting to Commander

Berto. I'm not even sure they're army. Look, some of them are wearing blue jeans and T-shirts. They might be from another faction."

Realizing that Melchor made sense, Danny said, "Helen, we need to go this way."

Knowing that the people shooting at them would emerge from the trees as soon as the smoke lifted, Danny looked up at the sun's position in the sky and turned the compass dial on his watch. Orienting himself back toward the direction they came, he pointed to the path leading out of the forest.

From behind the woods, Danny heard loud footsteps scuffing the earth and getting near them. Melchor pulled out his gun and started firing in the general direction of the ghostlike movements coming up from the bushes.

Out of the corner of his eye, Danny was shocked to see a man he hadn't seen since graduate school. The man stood at six foot five, with a head of thick gray hair and pale alabaster skin. This was the mentor that had sparked Danny's interest in the world's oceans. But unfortunately, he had also tried to destroy his career and in the process break him into a thousand pieces. This was the man who had taken him and Blake to court over the possession of the Rx-18 compound. Everything now made sense. Dr. Klein, his old teacher, wanted the compound for himself.

Danny, Helen and Melchor started running downhill.

DR. KLEIN AND HIS MEN emerged from the trees

looking for Danny. With the smoke lifting, he sprinted toward Danny as he towed the rollaway. Just as he was getting closer, he heard the popping sounds of a discharging gun. He fell down to the ground. A bullet hit a rock next to him and created a spark.

"Stay down until it's clear," Dr. Klein ordered his men.

After twenty minutes, the sea wind blew the smoke away and visibility returned to near 100 percent. Dr. Klein got up and began searching for Danny and his party.

"Look for footprints and find out where the fuck they ran!" Dr. Klein commanded.

His hired goons and ragtag mercenaries fanned out and searched the ground for footprints.

WITH THE SUN BEGINNING TO SET, the thick canopies of tree leaves formed broad shadows on the ground. It became difficult to navigate through the decreasing light. Danny checked the compass dial on his watch again. He remembered going uphill on the way to the rendezvous point with Vincent and his men. Going downhill, he was assured that he would get back to the Jeepney driver waiting for them.

"*Susmaryosep!*" Melchor said, raising his hand. "Hold up."

"What's he saying?" Helen asked.

"It's an expression—'Jesus, Mary, Joseph,'" Danny said. "Let's stop here for a moment."

Danny helped Melchor sit on a tree lying on the ground

and checked to see if any bullets or fragments of shrapnel had hit him. Helen moved closer to check his back and the side of his torso.

"I don't see bullet marks," Helen said.

"My stomach hurts so bad," Melchor said, his face grimacing in pain.

"You need to lie down for a moment," Helen said.

Melchor took several deep breaths to calm his nerves. Danny handed him their water bottle and he took a couple of swigs. After a few minutes, Melchor calmed down and his rapid breathing returned to normal.

"We need to go. This place will be crawling with soldiers soon," Melchor said, getting up.

DANNY WAS RELIEVED to see their driver anxiously standing by the Jeepney, still waiting for them.

"We need to take him to the hospital now," Helen said as she approached the driver.

Not wasting a second more, the driver put Melchor's arm around his shoulder and gently laid him on the long bench in the back.

"Let's go," Danny said.

With the setting sun already sinking in the western sky, it became increasingly difficult to drive through the island's unpopulated area. It was dark on the two-lane asphalt road. The driver flipped the Jeepney's headlights on. The faint yellow light pushed out against the dark night in front of them.

"Did you say excuse me three times while you were crossing the open field?" the driver asked, his eyes fixated on the road.

Helen was mystified with the driver's comment. "Why would we say that? There wasn't anybody else there."

"Of course there was! There are *Nuno sa Punso* living in the mound on the open field. He might have stepped on a Nuno and now he is pissed off and has cast a spell."

"What's he talking about, Danny?" Helen asked.

"Some of the people around here still believe that spirits freely roam the lands as soon as night falls. A Nuno is a dwarf, an old man with a long beard. Bad things could happen to the person who offends him."

"We're capable of sending tourists up in space, but people still believe in that?"

Danny heard Melchor moaning in pain and turned to him. His skin was getting paler by the minute. Helen placed his head on her lap, picked up the water bottle, poured its contents in a white cloth, and placed it on the Professor's forehead to comfort him.

"How far are we from the hospital?" Danny asked.

"A few more miles," the driver replied.

"No...no hospital," Melchor interrupted. "The army and the police might be waiting for us there. They will detain us if they find out we were involved in the shootout earlier."

"We need to do something," Helen said.

"I know an *albularyo,* a medicine man who lives close

by. Maybe he could do something," the driver said.

THE DRIVER PARKED THE JEEPNEY in front of the albularyo's house. It was a small house with a corrugated roof and unpainted cinder block walls. Danny and Helen assisted the professor off the Jeepney.

The driver knocked hard on the front door. A man in his late fifties with a thinning hairline and a mouth with half of his teeth missing answered. The driver spoke to him in a local dialect Danny couldn't understand.

"Let's take him in," the driver said.

The albularyo disappeared into the kitchen. A few minutes later, he came back with a washbasin, a long candle and a metal spatula.

"Does he really know what he's doing?" Helen asked.

Danny just shrugged his shoulders in response.

The albularyo took Melchor's shirt off and examined his stomach. His face quickly contorted into an expression of disappointment and worry. With broken Tagalog, he asked Melchor where he had been.

"I was just on the other side of the island near the mountain."

The albularyo said that Melchor might have stepped on a Nuno and that offering food and drinks might appease the spirit. Since there were several Nunos roaming the island, he needed to know which one. He erected the candle on the table, lit it and placed the metal spatula over the flame. When the metal spatula was glowing red hot, he blew out the flame, picked up the candle and pressed it on the metal spatula. The melted wax dripped into the water in the washbasin. An unrecognizable figure formed in the water. The albularyo was muttering something to himself as he attempted to interpret the mystery taking shape. After he was sure that he knew what was in front of him, he turned to Melchor and told him what he saw.

"What's he saying?" Helen asked, turning to Danny.

"The albularyo knows which Nuno Melchor stepped on and will recite special prayers, and ask the Nuno to forgive Melchor by offering him food and water."

The albularyo closed his eyes, held Melchor's hands and muttered some undistinguishable words. From the gist of what he was doing, Danny could tell that he was communicating to the spirit that Melchor had offended. When he was done a few minutes later, he offered a combination of rolled-up herbs and asked Melchor to chew it to help relieve his pain.

AFTER LEAVING A PACK of cigarettes and a few hundred pesos, they left the medicine man's house as soon as the ceremony was finished.

The driver drove cautiously, trying not to speed and hoping to avoid getting stopped by the military patrolling the streets. Melchor's pain was subsiding through the power of the herbs. His skin had returned to its normal dark brown color and his lips, ashen just a few hours ago, were back to their light pinkish tone.

"I don't trust the hospital here, so don't bother taking me there. I'm not going to get butchered here."

"You need medical attention," Danny pleaded.

"I'd rather take the chance flying two hours back to Manila and get the best care," Melchor said.

"What are your plans now, Melchor?" Danny asked.

"We should be in Manila by 10 o'clock tonight. You'll stay in a hotel and I'll ask my pilot to fly you directly to Tawi-Tawi in the morning."

"We don't know anyone there. How're we going to find Commander Berto and his men?" Helen asked.

"I've done some business with a councilman in Tawi-Tawi. He owes me a favor for developing one of his beach properties into a resort. He's a good man and a former officer in the army. He will help you find Blake," Melchor responded.

"Do you think that a councilman would know where he is? If the military couldn't locate him, how could he?" Danny asked.

"There are a lot of things you don't know about how things work around here. Everyone knows pretty much where everyone is. If he does not know where Commander Berto's hideout is, I'm sure he has people who can locate him."

"Why do we need to get him involved?" Helen asked. "What's in it for him?"

"Because we need a go-between. We need to reestablish some trust with Commander Berto. Popoy Arevalo is one of the richest guys in the area and was one of the leaders who helped arrange the release of a Frenchman who was abducted while scuba diving near the Balabac Islands."

"What if he doesn't want to get involved?" Helen asked.

"More likely he will help you. He's not stupid and he'll get something from this deal."

"If he refuses?" Danny asked.

"Then I have no choice but to text Commander Berto's messenger and, hopefully, he still trusts me after what happened in the forest and will meet with you. But that would be a long shot."

Danny felt the Jeepney decelerating. He peeked outside and saw several military armored personnel carriers blocking the road.

"Looks like there's a checkpoint up ahead," Danny said.

"Helen, cover your head so we don't raise any suspicion," Melchor said.

Helen dug in her bag until she found a scarf, hurriedly concealing the sides of her cheeks and folding the scarf's ends around her neck. Wanting to hide part of his face, Danny searched his immediate area, found a straw hat on the front passenger side and quickly placed it on his head.

As soon as the Jeepney stopped at the long bamboo barricade, the soldier sitting on top of the armored personnel carrier directed the bright lights at them. Danny raised his hand to shield his face. A soldier with an M-16 rifle, wearing a military fatigue uniform, peered inside. Danny bowed his head down and Helen avoided eye contact.

"Is everything all right here?" the soldier asked, sticking his head in the Jeepney while pointing the flashlight in their faces. "Where are you guys going?"

"Boss man," the driver replied, "I just took these guys to the albularyo, a few miles up that way. They heard about his mystic powers and we're just coming back after getting treatments."

With Melchor grimacing, he didn't have to exaggerate the pain in his face.

The soldier walked towards the back of the Jeepney, bent down and searched the open spaces under the seats. He swept the flashlight side to side looking for weapons and contraband. Helen pulled the scarf forward to conceal her exposed light skin cheeks. Danny's throat felt dry and he worried about the gun in the bag next to him. If the soldier found it, they could spend the night in jail or worse.

After a few tense moments that felt like an eternity, the soldier switched the flashlight off, not seeing anything out of the ordinary. He tapped the side of the Jeepney a couple times and signaled a soldier with a machine gun sitting on top of his armored personnel carrier to let them through. The driver shifted the gear to first and slowly rolled away.

Danny finally breathed a sigh of relief.

NEARING THE CITY CENTER with the checkpoint far behind them, Melchor reached for the radio scanner inside his bag and turned it on. The chatter on the radio was nonstop. They listened intently but it was difficult to discern whether the Philippine National Police or the local officials were talking as their sentences came out in quick bursts. Then the next message sent shivers up Danny's spine.

An all-points bulletin was being broadcasted: "Be on the lookout for a Caucasian female with two male companions. May be armed and dangerous."

"Damn! Everyone is looking for us," Danny said.

"Who sold us down the river?" Helen asked.

"I'm pretty sure that the people who fired on us earlier weren't the military," Danny said.

"Why would you say that?" Melchor asked.

"Because I saw Dr. Klein."

Helen and Melchor's faces immediately contorted into puzzled looks as if they couldn't comprehend what Danny was talking about.

"And?" Helen asked.

"He is my old professor who has been after the Cube for years. I believe he's here and wants it for himself."

"This complicates things. Not only are the police looking for us but also your Dr. Klein. If we're not able to deliver the money and the Cube to Commander Berto, he might kill Blake. Forget about our original plan. We can't go back to the airport together. Someone might already be waiting for us," Melchor said.

"What are you planning now?" Danny asked.

"Do you want us to stay here overnight and wait for the airplane to return in the morning and then fly to Tawi-Tawi?" Helen asked.

"That's too risky. I don't trust anyone here. I think there's a regularly-scheduled boat that goes to Tawi-Tawi."

"You sure?" Helen asked.

Melchor turned to the driver to confirm his assumption. "Is that right?"

"Yes. Every night," the driver said.

Four

THE SHIP'S ENGINES were already revving when they arrived at the pier. Danny climbed down from the Jeepney's rear exit with his rollaway bag, Helen following behind him.

Danny studied the ship that would take them all the way to Tawi-Tawi and contemplated whether to abort or to press on to see what was on the other side. He felt a slight uneasiness as he gazed at the women with long headscarves accompanied by men with brimless white caps. Danny wondered if he was doing the right thing by meeting Commander Berto on his own. Maybe it would be better to just turn around and let the Philippine authorities rescue Blake. He feared the potential for disaster was just too great. What could he do anyway? He was just an oceanographer and not some kind of superhero who can save the day and return everything back to the way it was.

"Are we doing the right thing?" Helen asked with doubt in her voice.

A part of him wanted to tell her to turn around, go straight to the Jolo airport and fly back to Manila. Their task was daunting and dangerous. He doubted that going to Tawi-Tawi, a place he had never heard of until today, would result in in Blake's release. He felt little control over the series of events that seemed to get worse with each passing hour. Coming to Mindanao was supposed to have been simple. He was supposed to meet with Commander Berto, give him what he wanted, and then fly back to Manila with Blake. Now, faced with another island to go to, he thought of Odysseus wandering in the Greek islands and taking years to get back home. Dr. Klein could already be one step ahead of him and waiting for his arrival in Tawi-Tawi. But he had no choice and couldn't trust anyone to take care of his personal business. Like a moth attracted to a lamp's light, all he could do was to fly right through the flame and hope he'd come out on the other side with Blake freed from his captors.

Danny took a deep breath and studied the ship's decks overloaded with passengers and cargoes. He wondered which would kill them first if things went wrong. Would it be the flimsy-looking ship sinking in the middle of the Sulu Sea or a bullet to the chest from Dr. Klein prowling in the periphery? Just thinking about it made his head throb in pain. Though he feared the possibility of either outcome, his anxiety at the thought of losing Blake was even greater.

"Bahala na," Danny replied, as he took a deep breath of the moist salty sea air.

"Huh?" Helen asked.

"Let fate decide."

Danny climbed up the ramp leading to the passenger ship.

AS THE SHIP PULLED AWAY from the pier, Danny and Helen searched the upper deck for a place to lay their tired bodies but were disappointed when they discovered that most of the cots were already occupied. Since they bought their tickets at the last minute, they were issued a "chance passenger" status, which meant that they could get on but were not guaranteed an available cot. After searching the entire ship, they found two empty cots side by side, next to stacks of rice sacks and caged chickens at the back of the boat. Danny threw his knapsack on the cot and laid down.

Going to Tawi-Tawi had never even crossed his mind, and now Danny found himself on a ship rolling along the choppy Sulu Sea on a starless night. He tried to wrap his mind around the fact that Dr. Klein was involved with Blake's kidnapping and how he got involved with Commander Berto. He opened his eyes and the bright, circular fluorescent lights momentarily blinded him. He noticed a lizard crawling on the ceiling. Did the lizard know which way is up and which way is down? He wondered why Dr. Klein was shooting at the members of the Kulog ng Timog.

He turned toward Helen who was sitting on the next cot and already making friends with a young girl and her mother. The girl was practicing her English with Helen.

"It's pronounced *apple*, not *eepol*," Helen remarked.

The little girl covered her mouth in an embarrassed giggle.

Aware that Danny was staring at her, Helen turned toward him. His dark chestnut eyes locked with the ocean of light inside her own. He thought of the last time they were together…

On a late summer afternoon, Danny was standing at the ferry terminal waiting for Helen to arrive. It had been a year since he saw her last. The wind blowing from the bay was cool on his face and the anticipation of seeing her lightened his heart. Out of the group of people walking in his direction, he spotted her right away with two cups of coffee in her hands. He walked up to her and she offered him one of the cups. He leaned forward and lightly kissed her on the lips. He realized how much he missed her presence.

They boarded the ferry to Coronado Island. While on the boat, Helen mentioned that she had just finished her teaching credential program and was considering a position offered to her. Danny said that research for the Cube had taken up most of his time.

Not having a concrete itinerary, they rode around town in a pedicab as the cool breeze stroked their faces. After deciding on the outdoor restaurant, they sat at the table under the canopy of the night sky, dotted with twinkling stars. Danny ordered wood-fired pizza—barbecued chicken flavor.

After dinner, they decided to stroll the shops on the main street. At one point, they passed by a jewelry store where a two-carat diamond ring was proudly displayed in the window. Danny noticed Helen's eyes fixed on the stone glistening under the lights. Danny wanted to buy the ring for her—he was sure she'd be happy but he knew that the time wasn't right to make a huge commitment. The Cube was his priority and the last thing he wanted was to ask Helen to sacrifice her career for him by staying in San Diego. Especially now that she had just become a credentialed teacher.

WITH THE SHIP SLIGHTLY oscillating with the waves, the ceiling lights turned off except for the dim lights along the aisles and the main deck finally quiet, Danny's nerves finally settled.

"How did this happen to us?" Helen asked, turning to Danny from her cot.

"I don't know. One moment we were madly in love, then we woke up one day and we weren't talking anymore," Danny replied.

"Did I do something to hurt your feelings?" she asked.

"No. I'm the one to blame. If I hadn't been so obsessed about trying to discover this damn Cube, we would have been living together a long time ago. Look what it has done to us."

"I guess I was partly to blame, too. I should have been a bit more flexible and returned to San Diego to be with you. I could have taught at the first school district that would hire me, even if it wasn't the salary I desired. At least I could have been with you," Helen replied.

Danny looked away from her. He noticed the girl and her mother were eating a late-night snack of sticky rice cakes, deep fried peanuts and hard-boiled eggs.

"I'm really sorry for destroying what we had."

"We're both to blame," Helen replied.

"When this is all over..." Danny said, reaching for her hand.

Helen did not take her hand away. It was the gesture she had been wanting from him for a long time. He gently stroked her hand. A tiny smile formed at the corner of her mouth. Danny felt the heavy weight of guilt lift off his chest. He was about to say something when he felt the vibration of the ship's engines decrease.

"Are we slowing down?" Helen asked.

Danny stood up and looked out across the open sea to check what was going on. Out in the distance, a beam of floodlights blinded him from a fast-approaching boat coming toward them. He turned to Helen who was also fixated on the bright lights.

"A small craft is approaching us."

"What's going on?" Helen asked.

"Dr. Klein has probably tracked us here and bribed some of the local officials."

Danny feared that the event was a repeat of what happened to Blake a few days earlier. Since the ship's crew was unarmed, a boat full of goons could easily get on board and take them away. If his fears were true, no one could help them.

The bright fluorescent lights on the deck came on.

As the boat slowly moved closer to the ship, Danny noticed the red, white and blue stripe on the bow.

"Isn't that the Coast Guard?" Helen asked.

The soldiers from the boat threw a grappling hook to the ship and pulled it in until the two sides of the crafts were touching each other. One by one, four soldiers hopped onboard balancing rifles on their shoulders.

The passengers who were already sleeping on the open cots were awakened by the sudden commotion. Danny peered toward the middle of the deck and noticed two Marines in full camouflage with ammunition belts and M-16s, walking with the ship's crew and asking passengers for their tickets. The other two Marines were poking and prodding with their rifles as they looked through the sacks of sugar, flour, and large cans of biscuits crowding the aisles.

An old man in the middle aisle was told to open the box by his cot. Danny feared that the Marines might ask him to open his luggage. If that happened, he wouldn't be able to explain the sealed packs of clay. The Marines might take it away thinking it was some sort of plastic explosive.

"It looks like they're coming toward us. Put your scarf over your head and let me do the talking just in case."

Two expressionless Marines approached them. The ship's employee asked for their tickets. Danny fished his ticket from his front pocket and Helen retrieved her ticket from her knapsack.

While the employee checked their tickets, Danny noticed one of the Marines looking down at Helen's brown hair.

Speaking in broken English, the Marine asked, "You with American woman?"

"Yes. She's my wife," Danny replied. "We're going scuba diving."

The Marine stared down at him with resentment for having to protect Western tourists like them. He and his fellow Marines risked their lives patrolling the seas all day and night to make the islands safe for everyone, while people like them came to spend more money in one day than he makes in a month.

"It isn't safe for tourists here. Go back to Manila right away when you're done with your business," the Marine said, walking away.

Done with their inspection, the Marines returned to the patrol boat. The tether was disengaged and the boat pulled away into the open sea.

BACK AT THE JOLO AIRPORT, Dr. Klein sat inside the four-door blue car with his men, patiently waiting for Danny to arrive.

"Which airplane did they arrive in?" Dr. Klein asked, turning to one of his men, a bald-headed, stocky-framed thug who had been staking out the planes all day.

"The twin engine parked by the terminal."

"We need to get to Danny before he gets on that plane or I'll never get a chance to get my hands on the damn Cube," Dr. Klein said to him. "Get out there and position yourselves around the airport and get ready to nab him when they arrive."

A Jeepney drove past Dr. Klein's car. He watched the driver get out, walk toward the back and assist a man he didn't recognize who was walking with a slight limp and clutching the side of his torso as he headed straight to the airplane. Dr. Klein reached for his phone and texted his men to stay alert and watch out for Danny.

"Fucking shit! Where the fuck is he hiding?" Dr. Klein muttered to himself.

Frustrated, he called one of his men, eyeing Rodriguez as he boarded the airplane.

"Is he carrying a large item?"

"No, just a small bag," the bald-headed goon answered. "Do you want us to stop him?"

"No. Don't make a move. There are soldiers all over the place. We might get detained for questioning if we're seen with guns. I don't think he has what I want. Take a picture of the airplane's tail number, then get back here," Dr. Klein said.

Back in the car, his bald-headed assistant asked Dr. Klein what to do next.

"I think Danny and the woman he's with are either hiding somewhere or have already left the island," Dr. Klein replied with frustration. "Let's go to the pier and check on the scheduled ships."

THERE WERE NO SHIPS at the pier when Dr. Klein and his men arrived. The pier was eerily quiet, lit by sparse incandescent light bulbs mounted on poles along the wharf. He saw two dockworkers sitting on the pier's wood planks smoking cigarettes.

"Excuse me," Dr. Klein said.

"If you're looking for a ride out of here then you're out of luck. Two boats just left a half hour ago. You've just missed them," one of the dockworkers answered.

"Where are they heading?" Dr. Klein asked.

"One was headed towards Zamboanga City and the other to Tawi-Tawi."

"We got separated with our friends. Do you recognize these people?" Dr. Klein showed Danny and Helen's pictures on his phone to the dockworkers. As part of his early surveillance, Klein had paid a man to spy on them at the Manila airport, snapping their pictures.

"I remember them. They came running up the

gangplank in a hurry."

"Do you remember which boat they boarded?" Dr. Klein asked.

The dockworkers looked at each other and scratched their heads.

"We don't really know. The ships were next to each other."

"When will the boat arrive in Zamboanga City?"

"Tomorrow around six in the morning."

"What about the one heading to Tawi-Tawi?"

"About the same time."

A smug smile oozed across Dr. Klein's face.

"WIFE, HUH?" Helen teased, grinning.

"I had to think real fast. I didn't like the way that soldier was looking at you. I'd kick his ass if not for the M-16 hanging on his shoulder," Danny replied.

"You're jealous."

"A little," Danny replied as he lay down on the cot.

"Do you remember that night when a drunk guy grabbed me at a party thinking I was his girlfriend?"

"Oh yeah. I almost got into a fight."

"You pushed him away so fast. I was in awe of what you were going to do for me."

"Luckily, there wasn't a pair of sticks nearby or I would have wacked him on the head."

"You'd really do that for me?"

"Perhaps…"

"I remember you took my hand and led me out of the house."

"How could I forget that night? I didn't know where to take you so I just kept driving until we ended up on the beach and made out all night," Danny said.

As the propellers pushed the boat to Tawi-Tawi, it churned out white froth, streaming behind the ship like a bridal veil. The steady hum from the ship's engine shook the deck. Danny wondered if the time was right to ask Helen to take him back and promise to make everything right again for both them. He was only a cot away from her but he couldn't muster the courage to tell her that he still loved her. He kept what he wanted to say to himself, turned to his side and closed his eyes.

Five

DANNY AWOKE TO THE SOUNDS of shuffling feet, muffled voices, and distant guitar chords. The morning sun hovered low on the horizon, filling the gaps between the large boxes and sacks of rice with orange light. He rubbed the thick film from his eyes and turned toward Helen's cot to find it empty. Worried that something might have happened, he sat up and scanned the immediate area. The passengers on the ship were all awake and walking around the shifting deck to wake up their stiff muscles. As he looked behind some kids playing hide and seek near the luggage, he was glad to see Helen walking slowly back. She held a box top as a tray with their breakfast, trying to avoid the kids trying to run into her.

"I got us some something to eat," Helen said, setting the tray on her cot.

Danny glanced down and saw several hot *pandesal*

(bread rolls) along with hard-boiled eggs and two cups of coffee. He picked up the cup and took several sips. The instant coffee's bitterness and the evaporated milk's sweetness tickled the tip of his tongue.

"You slept like a baby last night," Helen said.

"I was so tired. What time is it anyway?" Danny asked, taking a bite of bread.

"It's just past six."

"Wouldn't waffles doused in maple syrup, bacon, and two eggs sunny-side up be great? This food reminds me of camping when I was a boy."

"I think you have to wait until we get back to the States for that. You'll just have to settle with the local treats," she said, taking a bite of her bread.

"I guess I just have to wait and hopefully, Blake will be joining us for our next breakfast."

"Dr. Klein won't stop until he intercepts us and gets the Cube," she said as she wiped the corners of her mouth with the back of her hand.

"That's why we need to get to Commander Berto before he gets to us."

"Do you think some rich guy is helping him? His private army must have cost a lot."

"I was thinking the same thing. A year ago, Blake and I sent a description of the Cube's formula to several companies hoping for sponsors to continue funding our project. We described its basic makeup but not everything about it," Danny said.

"Why would he go through all the trouble to get the Cube away from you?"

"Maybe he figured out a new use and wants to push me and Blake out."

"He could have easily built his own compound. He knows the formula," Helen said.

"It's more complicated than that. Blake and I worked on it for years and only recently unlocked how to make it work properly."

"But you've sent out the basic formula. Can't anyone recreate it?"

"Remember when we spent that weekend in San Francisco? When we sat in the park and ate buttered sourdough bread?"

"Of course."

"To make bread, all you need are flour, water, salt and yeast. And yet, no one can make that same authentic sourdough taste from the bakery at the Fisherman's Wharf. It's the same concept. The Rx-18 compound's basic formula has been around for years. Every budding scientist has been taking a crack at it, but no one has been successful."

"OK…but nothing quite makes sense. He can't just peddle the compound you discovered. You'll just go after him with a lawsuit," she said, trying to sound hopeful.

"Blake and I haven't had time to patent the latest batch because we were tweaking it as we went. I think Dr. Klein knows that we've deviated far from our original patent and that's why he wants to get his hands on the Cube. He knows what we're up to and maybe he discovered something that Blake and I aren't aware of."

"Why do you think he's also intent on getting the Cube?"

"That's what's so puzzling about this whole thing. He knows the formula Blake and I were using. He discovered some of its initial building blocks and suggested a few changes."

Helen shifted her gaze toward the ocean, trying to make sense of all the confusion around her.

"Before your unfortunate parting with Dr. Klein, were you already at the stage where the Cube could attract fish?" Helen asked.

Danny moved his face closer to Helen as if he was worried that someone might hear his revelation.

"Of course. That's the easy part. The problem with the Cube is that it's great at attracting fish but it's not selective. You liked feeding the fish in my aquarium whenever you visited my apartment right?"

"Yes. What's your point?" She said, her eyebrows colliding in the middle of her face.

"The fish came rushing to the falling flakes and then twenty seconds later, after all of them were full, the fish slowly began losing interest and started to swim away. It's the same concept. What Blake and I are trying to do is to lure specific fish—like certain species of tuna that might go extinct due to overfishing in the coming decades—and make them follow a ship while feeding all the way to the protected waters. If we can keep them there where commercial fishing is not allowed, we could save the species."

Helen paused for a moment, trying to process Danny's explanation. She thought about the lonely nights she spent in her apartment while Danny was in the lab perfecting the Cube. A strange feeling came over her. Instead of harboring resentment for how he neglected her, she felt a twinge of admiration in his revelation. He was helping to save the world—one species at a time.

"Now I understand why you were in such a race against the clock. It looks like you're running out of time. The fish population is being depleted every day," Helen said.

"We've been hard at work on it for four years and still haven't achieved truly promising results. We track the fish with sonars but after ten miles or so the fish we want lose interest and scatter. The Cube is still highly unstable and has too many flaws with its design. Plus, if you add the fickle nature of ocean temperatures and the unpredictable fish migration patterns, it's hard to make it work."

"Maybe Dr. Klein found out about a different use for your latest variation?" Helen asked.

"That's the horrible side of this invention. If it falls into the greedy hands of a commercial fishing company, it might just mean the end of all fish species. But I'm not worried about that for now—unless Dr. Klein had learned something new."

"How did you meet him?" Helen asked, eagerness in her voice.

Danny looked Helen in the eye, then said, "I might as well tell you how I also met your cousin."

Danny began to narrate.

"I saw Dr. Klein when he walked into my chemistry class as our instructor in my first semester of graduate school. He was an imposing man who commanded your full attention when he talked. He made sure that the assigned experiments were done properly according to the instructions at the workstations. Though he was strict, he was funny and encouraged all his students who came to his lab to perform their best. His thin physique along with his black, plastic prescription glasses gave the impression the he was knowledgeable in science.

Dr. Klein approached me about a side project he was working on but had no time to complete. The project centered on researching the tide pools along the coast. Helping him with the project would count as extra credit and since I needed to boost my grade, I agreed. He introduced me to Blake and we clicked right away. I liked your cousin and I could tell he was fond of me, too.

One day after class, Dr. Klein invited me and Blake to a local Irish pub near the university. While having a glass of cold beer, he told us about the grave situation of the world's fish population, about its depletion due to overfishing, and how the world's governments had no policy or program in place to replenish the marine life lost each day. He was the one who first explained to us how marine life could not reproduce fast enough to keep pace with commercial fishing. It was back in that pub, with its noisy patrons and beer-stained floor, that Blake and I realized what we needed to do.

Immediately after finishing graduate school, Blake and I became obsessed with saving the ocean's fish population. We came across an article describing the protected areas in the ocean where commercial fishing is forbidden and we had an idea. What if we could move some of the ocean's marine life to those protected waters? And what if we could keep the endangered marine life there so no one could touch them? But in order to do that, we knew we needed a way to attract the fish to the protected areas.

So Blake and I began experimenting with different food sources from other fish and plants. Our goal from day one was to create a type of food agent that would attract fish to migrate toward the protected areas that are banned from fishing, where the fish would have a chance to spawn, thrive and multiply. We were going to replenish the fish population so the next generation could also enjoy the bounties of the sea.

It took time and dedication but we finally came up with a viable compound that produced a reliable result. Blake and I patented the Rx-18 compound and nicknamed it 'the Cube' because of its shape when molded. When Dr. Klein found out about our work, he immediately demanded 50 percent of the patent rights due to the scientific advice he had given us through the years. He took us to court and after a year of motions and a trial it was deemed his suggestions were purely academic and could have been found in any number of already published journals. The court ultimately decided he wasn't entitled to any part of our patent. We thought that was the end but then he began a quest to destroy our reputations by claiming we were a pair of quack scientists."

ONE OF THE BOAT'S ATTENDANTS was walking on the deck, shouting to the passengers that they had arrived at their destination and should prepare to disembark. Curious, Danny looked out at the railing. He could see the outline of Tawi-Tawi's capital, Bongao. Houses built on stilts crowded along the waterfront. Yellow-hulled passenger boats were pulling away from the docks. Helen moved closer to him. As their ship came closer to the capital, he saw the top of the mosque's white, onion-shaped dome rising behind several houses. Getting closer to the docks, the fresh rising sun bathed the streets, turning the clumps of tall-legged houses into a tangerine-colored city.

Concerned that Dr. Klein and his men might be waiting by the exit, Danny walked over to the ship's port side and scanned the immediate area. The passengers were going down the ramp, towing large boxes containing clothes and household items. Porters stood on the docks puffing cigarettes while waiting for the signal for the cargo to be unloaded. Next to the parked pickup trucks and motorcycles, Danny spotted four men in blue jeans and polo shirts. One of them stood out, his hair combed back, a tent-shaped moustache and a pistol bulging on his hip.

"Looks like our welcoming party is already here," said Danny fear rising in his voice.

Helen narrowed her eyes as she confirmed Danny's description. "Everyone here seems to carry guns. They could just be plainclothes police."

"I don't like the way they look. See that barrel-chested guy with the ugly-looking moustache?"

"The one with the cat's-eye sunglasses?" Helen whispered.

"Yup. I think they're watching everyone going down the ramp," Danny said, already searching for a way to circumvent the men waiting for them.

"How are we going to get through them? I'm sure those men already know how we look."

"The only exit is through the main ramp and I don't think we can muscle our way out."

"Maybe we can approach the military jeep and ask the soldiers to escort us out."

Danny contemplated Helen's suggestion. Though it made sense, it was only a temporary solution. "Even if the soldiers agreed to accompany us out, those men will follow us and then nab us as soon as we're dropped off."

Danny toyed with the idea of blending in with the crowd and disappearing once they reached the main street, but with more than half of the passengers already off the ship, the chances that they would be spotted were rapidly increasing. Danny had to think fast on how to evade them.

"We'll stay here until everyone has cleared out. Maybe they'll give up and leave." Danny hoped his plan would work.

"They know we're aboard. Eventually they will be, too, and won't stop looking for us until the last square inch of each deck is checked," Helen said, panic vibrating in her voice.

Desperate to find a way to evade the men waiting for them, Danny looked around for yet another way to get down. "Cover your head with the scarf and try to hide as much of your face as possible. I think I found a way out of here," Danny said, donning a pair of sunglasses.

They lowered their heads as they squeezed themselves among the impatient passengers as they waited for their turn to get down. They proceeded directly to the ramp attached to the back of the ship. Shirtless stevedores drenched in sweat walked hurriedly down the wooden incline with sacks of rice. Danny carried the rollaway on his right shoulder, trying to hide his face. Reaching the bottom of the ramp, he checked to see what the four suspicious men waiting for them were doing. Out of the corner of his eye, he saw the man with the tent-shaped moustache leading the charge and shoehorning his way in between the dockworkers walking toward the truck unloading boxes. Shivers ran down his spine. He and

Helen were already discovered.

"This way," Danny yelled through the noise of pickup trucks moving in and out of the docks.

Bongao's main street was teeming with activity. He saw motorized tricycles (motorcycles with sidecars) carrying passengers and zipping along the narrow streets. Children in dirty shirts were selling sweet rice wrapped in banana leaves and deep-fried brown-sugar yams on a stick. Food stalls lined the street, selling barbecued fish, squid and chicken. Danny and Helen found little comfort in the hustle and bustle swirling around them because they knew it was just a matter of time before the men lurking in the area would find them.

"Let's get in here and hide for a moment," Helen said as she urgently pointed to a small, family-owned variety shop, commonly called a *sari-sari* store, on the side of the road.

When they walked in the door, young boys and girls in their school uniforms were crowding the aisles buying their candies and corn chips. Cans of pork and beans and luncheon meat were stacked high along the wall. A woman sitting behind the cash register surrounded by bags of fried peanuts followed them with amused eyes.

Looking through the large window, Danny recognized the four men with their hurried steps and swiveling necks fanning across the street's length. Trapped in the sari-sari store, he placed his hand on Helen's shoulders and spun her out of their sight. Together they hid behind the stacked cases of soda bottles.

"They're over there," Danny said, lowering his voice fearing one of them might walk in and find them.

After a few tense minutes, Danny peeked through the window. The men were gone.

"How are we going to get in contact with the councilman?" Helen asked.

"I really don't know," Danny replied. "Melchor forgot to tell us what to do once we arrived here."

He turned his phone on and pressed Melchor's contact number, but only heard a squeaky out-of-service tone.

"Damn. My phone's not working."

"Your SIM card might not work here," Helen said, strutting toward the woman behind the counter.

After throwing in a new SIM card, Danny quickly entered Melchor's contact information. Danny pressed the phone to his ear eager to make contact, but the call transferred to voicemail.

"He's not answering," Danny said, dropping the phone in his front pocket, dejected and uncertain about what to do next.

"Do you think the councilman will help us?" Helen said, sounding frustrated.

They had risked life and limb coming to Tawi-Tawi, and if Popoy Arevalo refused to help them, it would be the end of the road for Blake's search. It was then that Danny and Helen realized that neither one of them had any viable plan on how to locate Commander Berto.

"We must find and convince him before Blake gets slaughtered by that animal," Danny replied, a new conviction in his voice.

"Sometimes politicians have different agendas. What if he doesn't even care about what we're going through?"

"We have no choice but to make it work," Danny said with grim determination.

As Danny moved toward the window to check if it was safe to leave, he noticed a faded, light-blue campaign poster tacked on the wall across the street. It featured a man with a wide grin standing in front of the provincial Capitol building. Below his picture was the caption: "Elect Arevalo."

Danny turned to Helen. "That's Arevalo in the picture! I think I know where to reach him."

THE CAPITOL, a whitewashed building, crowned with its onion-shaped dome, came into Helen's view through the motorized tricycle's tiny windshield as they trudged up the hill. The structure was grand—reminding visitors who entered the wide doors that powerful sultans once ruled these islands. With the large provincial seal displayed on the front, Danny knew he had come to the right place.

They climbed up the wide stairs and walked into the building. Helen thought it was odd that the front lobby was absent of the usual activity of people getting their affairs sorted by government officials.

"Looks like it's deserted," Helen remarked, peering in the hallways.

"This is strange," Danny muttered, already advancing toward the dim corridors lit only by the sunlight sprinkling through the windows.

"What kind of government building is this? It's a weekday and yet no one is around," Helen commented as the sound of her brisk footsteps reverberated off the walls.

AT THE END OF THE HALLWAY, Helen heard the keystrokes of a computer keyboard clacking out of an open door down the hallway.

"Let's ask the person inside," she said.

When they walked in, they saw a woman in a black headscarf with her head buried at the computer monitor. Helen cleared her throat to catch the woman's attention.

"May I help you?" the woman asked, looking alarmed.

"We're looking for Councilman Arevalo. Is it possible to see him?" Helen asked.

She smiled sarcastically. "He is a very busy man. You can't just walk in here without an appointment."

"It is very important that we talk to him," Helen replied, her voice steadily building with frustration.

"Take a number. You will be first in line as soon as he's done rooting out the radicals, feeding the hungry, setting up medical clinics—and I almost forgot—the people ahead of you asking for favors," the woman said with irritation.

"Ma'am," Danny said, in the most pleasing voice he

could. "We're here because…"

A dark-skinned, curly-haired man with a protruding stomach suddenly emerged from the adjacent room.

"Is there something I can do for you? I am one of the councilman's assistants. Call me Vic."

"Sir, I don't know if you've heard of the American who was kidnapped about a hundred miles from the Turtle Islands…"

"I'm aware of what happens in my own backyard."

"We're here to see Councilman Arevalo," Helen followed up.

"Who are you two?" Vic snapped. "I don't understand why you're here."

"I'm really sorry if we didn't introduce ourselves properly," Danny said, his head slightly bowed. "My name is Danny Maglaya. I'm a scientist from the United States. I work with the kidnapped victim. This is Helen Glass, the victim's cousin."

"Isn't he being held in Jolo Island? It's relatively peaceful here. Are you sure you're in the right place?"

"We were there yesterday to meet with the Kulog ng Timog but were ambushed. They ran to one of their hideouts in these parts and we were hoping that he could help us find them," Danny said.

"What makes you think that Popoy would know where that pest is hiding? The army has helicopters, night-vision goggles, and plenty of resources at their disposal to flush them out. They are better at locating him than we are," Vic replied.

"Sir, we need to reach Commander Berto to pay the ransom he demands. Professor Melchor Rodriguez sent a message to Councilman Arevalo and told him that we're coming. I believe the professor is his friend who was in charge of developing a resort," Danny said.

"How come he's not with you?" Vic asked, perplexed.

"He had to be flown back to Manila for a medical emergency," Helen added.

Vic crossed his arms, puffing up his chest as he processed what they were telling him. He gave Danny a cold hard stare. The silence was deafening as Vic decided what to do next. Helen shifted her weight from one leg to the other, worried that they would be back out on the street if Vic didn't believe their story or offer help. Vic unclipped his phone from his belt and dialed a number. After facing away from them, he started speaking at a rapid pace in a local dialect. Although Danny recognized bits and pieces of Tagalog, he couldn't understand what Vic was saying. Vic nodded his head whenever he heard something agreeable from the person on the other line.

"I just got off the phone with his secretary. Popoy Arevalo is already expecting you," Vic said, clipping the phone back on his hip. "Is it true that someone is after you?"

"A few hired mercenaries," Danny answered. "But we don't really know why." He decided to conceal Dr. Klein's involvement. The last thing he wanted was to complicate the situation.

"We need to take you to Popoy Arevalo's resort compound immediately for your own safety."

Six

A BLUE PICKUP TRUCK pulled in front of the Capitol carrying three men dressed in civilian clothes, armed with M-14 rifles. Vic walked down the steps and approached the vehicle.

"They're the councilman's bodyguards and will take you to his residential resort on the beach. He's on a nearby island right now, attending to his affairs and will be there this afternoon to meet the business leaders in the region. I'll see you there later."

Danny and Helen sat in the truck's bed next to a thin-framed twenty-something with wavy hair and a rifle between his legs. He introduced himself as Alex.

"Thanks for babysitting us," Helen said.

"No worries," Alex replied. "I enjoy meeting new guests."

While the wind blew in his face, Danny saw Mount

Bongao, home of the long-tailed macaques, rising in the distance. He imagined the cute monkeys jumping from tree to tree foraging for food.

Nearing the resort, beach houses built on stilts appeared in the distance. Residents sat outside with bored looks on their faces. An elderly woman sitting on the front steps of her house was combing a teenaged girl's hair. Kids in their rubber sandals dribbled a basketball on a dirt court, shooting the ball on a ring attached to a coconut tree trunk.

THE RESORT COMPOUND was empty when the pickup truck arrived. Danny jumped out of the vehicle while Alex helped Helen down.

"Wait here while I get someone to help you," Alex said, his rifle balanced on his shoulder.

Waiting on the grass, a slender young woman approached them. She had a clear, dark complexion and long, beautiful hair. She was wearing a long red skirt with a long-sleeved blouse.

"I'll be helping you while you're here. I'm one of the councilman's ten children. My name is Leilani, but you can call me Lei," she introduced herself with a smile that tugged at the corner of her mouth.

"Nice to meet you. I'm Helen and this is Danny."

Helen sounded grateful to see someone who was going to tend to their needs.

"Do you know what your father is planning for us?"

Danny asked.

"Unfortunately you came on one of our busiest days. My father instructed me to set you up for your night's stay," Lei said.

"Do you know when we could meet your father?" Danny asked.

"He usually meets with last-minute guests after he's done attending to the concerns of the businessmen on the island. His secretary knows you're here and I'm pretty sure he'll meet with you before the day is over. Let me show you where you'll be staying," Lei said, walking toward the bungalows built on stilts over the water.

Walking on the wooden planks leading to their room, Danny looked down into the crystal clear water. He couldn't have imagined that such a paradise existed. The overwater bungalows had bamboo walls, dried straw roofs and wide windows on both sides to let the cross breeze through.

"You'll be staying in that one right there," Leilani said, pointing to a bungalow with a built-in deck and a ladder that led down to the water. "Married couples love that one."

"We're not married," Helen replied, a hint of embarrassment in her voice.

"Oh, I'm sorry. I assumed right away. You looked so comfortable with each other," Lei said. "I guess I'll have to arrange separate cottages."

Danny walked inside his bungalow and pushed the

window covers open with a log stick. Exhausted from the overnight trip, he laid down on the *banig*—a stained, yellow straw mat scattered with a square pattern of red and purple on the floor and flattened his back. The wind blowing in from the Sulu Sea was refreshing. He closed his tired eyes and tried to push away any apprehension he had about meeting with Councilman Arevalo. The sound of the tides just below the floor soothed him. He thought about Vic's comment earlier. If the army couldn't locate Commander Berto, then how could a politician do it? But with the Councilman's willingness to meet with him, that was a good sign that something might get done. On the other hand, Arevalo might just pay lip service and give him the typical "I'll see what I can do" response.

He heard a light knock on the door. He lifted his wrist over his face to check the time. It was almost five in the afternoon.

"Come in."

When the door opened, Lei was standing outside with Helen who was wearing a *malong*—a tube-style cloth wrapped around her waist fashioned as a skirt.

"You might need a fresh change of shirt," Lei said, offering him a brown shirt.

"What do you call that? It looks amazing."

"*Batik*. It's a popular men's wear."

Danny took the shirt from her and held it up, inspecting its kaleidoscopic flower patterns of light mocha and dark coffee. He pulled the shirt he was wearing over his head and slipped the batik on.

"Fits perfect," Danny said, combing his hair with his fingers.

"My father is ready to see you now."

DANNY AND HELEN, accompanied by Lei, slowly and cautiously approached the councilman, sitting motionless on a wicker chair, looking out into the caramel-colored sky. Lei approached him and whispered something in his ear.

"Meet my father, The Honorable Popoy Arevalo," Lei said, backing away.

Councilman Arevalo was in his late forties with perfectly cut hair, distinguished by little wisps of grey along the sides.

Putting his hands together, bowing slightly, and feeling a tinge of intimidation at the former army colonel, Danny said, "Thank you for taking time out of your busy day to talk to us."

The councilman reached for the bottle of Fundador brandy resting on the table, poured it into his glass, tilted his head back, and chugged half of its contents in a single gulp.

"You two want a drink? It's calming after a stressful day," he said, raising the glass.

Danny contemplated what to say next. He was only an occasional drinker, and when he did drink, it was wine and never hard liquor. He was about to decline when the councilman interrupted him.

"I could tell you're not much of a drinker. I know liquor is bad for the liver but it's good for the soul!" He said, puckering his face after another swig.

Danny gave a light chuckle at the man's humor.

"We've heard you helped with the release of the kidnapped Frenchman two years ago?" Danny asked.

"I just played a small role. How are you related to the person kidnapped?" the councilman asked, looking straight at Danny and Helen. His eyes suddenly filled with intensity.

"We work together as scientists for a biotech company. Blake also happens to be my best friend, sir."

"What exactly do you do?"

"We're working on fish migration patterns and finding ways to save them from extinction so future generations will also have the chance to enjoy fresh sushi."

"Looks like you're doing good work. Some of the fishermen in the country are using dynamite to catch fish. They destroy reefs that took thousands of years for Mother Nature to build," he said, putting his empty glass on the table.

"The damage to the reefs is sometimes irreversible," Danny lamented.

"Unfortunately, there are a lot of uneducated people who don't care about the consequences of what they're doing. The fish collected looked horrible and unappealing. Eyes are popped out, carcasses are mangled, and the gills are sticking out. No one would want to buy a fish that looks like it had been chewed up and spat out by Godzilla."

"It's illegal, right?"

"Of course it is, but most fishermen who do it get away without getting in trouble because some of the public officials are easily bribed and there is a lack of enforcement."

Danny was shocked by the Popoy Arevalo's revelation. He never thought that any fishermen would carry out such a dangerous and destructive method of fishing.

"And who might you be?"

"Helen Glass. I'm the victim's cousin. I brought the money for Blake's ransom."

He turned his attention toward the beach and watched the small *banca* (a double outrigger) canoes floating by.

"Usually in kidnapping situations, once the ransom is transferred, the hostage is dropped off at an agreed-upon location. I don't understand why you want to get in touch with Commander Berto. Just wire the money to the account he gave you. It's too dangerous to try meeting with him."

"My uncle is paying for his release and wants proof of his life before wiring the money. The only way we could make a bank transfer is by having Blake's finger and my own scanned together," Helen added.

"Also, Commander Berto wants the research compound that Blake and I invented," Danny added. "It's also a condition for his release."

Councilman Arevalo put his fingers to his chin and narrowed his eyes as he thought through their situation.

"It doesn't make any sense. This is the first time I'd heard of such a request. Commander Berto and his ragtag band of thugs are nothing but a bunch of uneducated fishermen. What do they know about scientific inventions?"

"Is there a way we could establish contact through some back channel?" Helen asked.

"We might have a problem locating Commander Berto. He's most likely hiding out in any one of the hundreds of tiny islands around here. He has a strong network of well-paid informants that protect and alert him. He and his men are able to just get up and go, and escape in their powerful speedboats the moment they're alerted or detect a Coast Guard patrol boat is coming."

"Don't they usually hide in Basilan Island?" Helen asked.

"Yeah, but there are thousands of soldiers stationed there. I think they might have headed our way to avoid being seen. It will be hard to find them."

"Can you please help us find Blake so we can pay his ransom and take him back home?"

"If I could locate Berto's spider hole, I'd kill him myself. Men like him have caused so much trouble for my people," he said, frustration booming in his voice.

"Is there any way we could send the commander a

message that we have the compound and the money?" Danny asked.

"We're willing to meet him anywhere he wants," Helen added.

The councilman's dark brown eyes stared deeply into Danny's. The serious look on his face suggested that he was thinking about how he could help them.

"I'll see what I can do for you. I don't want your cousin to die on my watch. It wouldn't be good for anyone involved and I don't want anyone—especially an American—to get killed here and have the news media accusing me of doing nothing."

"Thank you so much, Mr. Arevalo," Helen said.

The councilman stood up from his chair. "I will send my people to make contact with Commander Berto as soon as possible. Meanwhile, please enjoy our island hospitality."

WHILE WALKING BACK to his bungalow on the water, Danny passed by Vic sitting with the councilman's bodyguards around a small table near a coconut tree.

"Danny, come over here and join us," Vic said.

His initial reaction was to refuse the invitation so he could be with Helen. All Danny wanted was to spend the early evening with her and maybe resolve some of the issues that had been plaguing them since their reunion back in Manila. He wanted to ask her if they could start seeing each other again once this nightmare was finally over and they were back in San Diego. The overnight trip from Jolo had rekindled feelings that had been dormant in his heart for years. But spending a few minutes with the men who'd be risking their lives to help rescue Blake wasn't too much to ask. The minimum he could do was to get to know them for a while. Walking away from Vic and his men might be construed as rude. Not wanting to offend his hosts, Danny turned to Helen and said, "Why don't you join Leilani at the gazebo. I need to sit with these guys so they won't think we're snobs."

"I'll talk to you later," Helen said, walking away.

DANNY ROLLED HIS SLEEVES up and sat near the men on a wooden bench.

"Just having a little fun in case we make contact with Commander Berto and have to get rolling right away," Vic said.

"I'm sorry that you have to be involved with our problem," Danny said.

"Nah…don't worry about it. We're doing this for our own people, too. We want the waters to be safe for everyone, not just outsiders. Please, have a drink of this *lambanog* coconut vodka with us."

"Yeah," Alex added. "Fuck Commander Berto and the boat he came in on. We'll blow him out of the water when we see him."

The rest of the guys laughed.

Vic poured a glass of lambanog. Swirling the liquor

until it created a small tempest, he then dumped it on the ground. Puzzled, Danny asked, "Why did you do that?"

"It's one of those traditions that makes no sense. It's supposed to be an offering for our departed drinking buddies and families," Vic said.

As one of the bodyguards filled the glass halfway with the clear liquid, the alcohol's strong smell wafted toward Danny. Vic offered him the first drink. Knowing the men might take it as an insult if he refused, he took the glass from Vic's hand, closed his eyes, tilted his head back, and took a swig. Almost immediately, he felt his sinuses clear as the 90-proof, distilled-coconut concoction flowed down his esophagus. Feeling dizzy, he thumped the glass on the table.

"It's like drinking jet fuel," Danny commented, his face turning red.

Using the same glass that Danny had just drank from, Alex poured more lambanog and passed it to Vic. He chugged the brew, his face not flinching, as if he were drinking ice-cold water on a hot summer day. The glass was passed around until everyone at the table drank the homemade spirit.

"Here, have some of this *pulutan*. It's an appetizer that makes drinking even more fun," Vic said.

Danny looked at a plate with several pieces of cubed beef on skewers in a bowl of red sauce.

"I bet you don't have that where you live. It's called *satti*."

Danny took a stick from the bowl and tried it. The taste of ginger, onion, tomato, turmeric, and several other spices that he couldn't identify mixed on his tongue. As he chewed the foreign-tasting barbecue, it immediately brought delight to his senses.

Danny shifted his gaze in Helen's direction to see if she was done talking to Lei.

"Your girlfriend is doing fine over there. No one is going to touch her," Vic said.

Danny quickly shifted his attention back to the bodyguards as they chuckled. He found it ironic that these hardened men who saw death and destruction in the type of work they did could also act like a bunch of high school teenagers when their guard was down.

"Just curious about what they're doing," Danny replied, half-embarrassed.

"Would you like to buy your lady friend a pearl ring?" Alex asked.

"I don't know. It never really crossed my mind."

"One of our guards works part time at the nearby pearl farm and brought in a ring he made. He was going to sell it to a jewelry store but asked me if you were interested."

Danny examined the glistening pearl perched on top of a silver ring and imagined it on Helen's finger.

"How much?" Danny asked.

"$200," Vic replied.

"I don't have that kind of money."

"You have a million dollars to pay for your friend," Vic

teased.

"Yeah…that's not my money. I'll pay a hundred. That's all I can afford."

Vic took Danny's hand and dropped the ring into it.

"OK, a hundred dollars. For an American boy, you know how to bargain like a fishmonger."

"There you go," Danny said, pulling out a one hundred dollar bill from his pocket and handing it to Vic.

WHILE THE MEN were merrily consuming the lambanog and getting tipsier by the minute, Danny quietly slipped away and headed toward his bungalow. He found Helen standing alone on the wooden plank and looking over the railing.

"Looks like you're lost in thought," Danny said, approaching her.

Helen turned around to face Danny.

He wanted to wrap his arms around her and to caress her like he had done in the past but couldn't find the courage to do so. Though he was only a few feet away from her, it felt like they were at opposite ends of the Sulu Sea. The thought of his past transgressions prevented him from making a move.

With their halted conversation showing signs of strain, neither one knew what to say next. After a few silent minutes, Danny was glad to see a firefly hovering next to them, blinking its faint green light in the dark night.

"I haven't seen one since I was a kid," Danny

commented, breaking the awkwardness."

"Do you know fireflies flash their light as part of their courtship?" Helen remarked.

"I also heard that they die two weeks after mating."

Danny reached for the lantern hanging on the window and intermittently blocked the light with his hand.

"Like this?" Danny asked.

"I think so."

"Can you read my message?"

"Can't tell. What's it about?" Helen answered playfully.

"More like it's getting late and we need some sleep. I'll see you in the morning." Danny said, turning toward his bungalow.

"Can you sleep in my room tonight?"

Her request caught him by surprise. His first reaction was to refuse. This wasn't the time to be alone with her...not yet. It might complicate matters just as they were beginning to mend the fences between them. There were so many issues from their informal breakup that hadn't been addressed. He worried that what might happen behind closed doors in a darkened room might destroy any chance of their truly becoming a loving couple again. But Danny recognized a hidden plea in her voice. It seemed that she wanted to tell him something that can only be said within the bamboo-latticed walls.

"Do you think it's a good idea?" he asked.

"I don't want to be alone surrounded by so many men with guns," she said.

DANNY HUNG THE LANTERN in the corner of the room. As the flame sputtered, their shadows outlined on the floor swayed from side to side. He spread his *banig* on the floor at the opposite side of the room and arranged the pillows and the thin red sheet.

In the hot and humid air, he took his shirt off, laid down on the banig, and placed his hands under his head. Helen stole a glance in his direction. The sight of the interweaving knots of muscles in his arms made her want to move across the room and lay down in the warmth of his embrace.

"I accepted a job offer in San Diego," Helen said. "And I'm moving back."

Danny was taken aback by her revelation. Helen was on the fast track in her career in Boston, and that she was willing to sacrifice that position was the last thing he expected to hear from her.

"I thought you enjoy teaching in Boston."

"Three years are long enough. Everybody I care about is in San Diego."

With the peace offering that Helen was extending, Danny knew that she was waving the white flag. He wanted to let her know that he was also tired of being alone and wanted to be with her.

"You will make a lot of people happy. Especially me."

A light breeze blew in from the ocean and carried the sweet scent of the *Dama de Noche* flower. Legend has it that the scent, only emitted at night, was from a heartbroken princess waiting for her prince to return.

Danny turned toward Helen. He thought of reaching for her hand, kissing her clear-skinned cheeks, and running his fingers through her light brown hair. But he couldn't find the courage to do it.

The continuous sounds of crickets chirping in the bushes mixed with the soft rumbling of the waves lapping on the shore rushed into the room.

Danny wondered if the scent was a sign that Helen still wanted him. With that thought, he closed his eyes and yearned to end their current dilemma. It was only with Blake's rescue that the two of them could get back to San Diego and attend to the pressing issue between them...love.

Seven

LOOKING OUT THE WINDOW, Danny saw the councilman's bodyguards gathered around a table as they cleaned their rifles and teased each other while drinking coffee with Vic. A Philippine Navy patrol boat was marooned on the beach. The sight of it concerned him. He wondered if asking for Popoy Arevalo's help was a good idea, considering he had expressed his desire to do away with Commander Berto. The last thing he wanted was a confrontation between the Kulog ng Timog and the military jeopardizing his mission to get Blake back. Peering toward the gazebo, he saw Helen, her hair neatly tied in a ponytail, having breakfast with Lei and several other women.

Wanting to find out the latest developments, he hurried toward Vic.

"Any news?" Danny asked with slight apprehension in

his voice.

"One of our informants just made contact with Commander Berto early this morning. He wants us to meet him at a fixed GPS coordinate in the middle of the ocean," Vic replied, looking down the pistol's sights. "I heard he wants you to test the compound in front of him before releasing Blake."

"Who are all these men with rifles? How come the military is here, too?" Danny asked.

"It's a two-in-one mission. After we get Blake on our boat and we've been safely separated, my men and I will go after Commander Berto and blow him out of the water."

"Aren't you concerned that things could go wrong? It's too risky. Why can't we just make the exchange and then leave?"

"We need to send a message to his supporters that they aren't welcome here to conduct their business."

The councilman approached the grassy area, flanked by two men in military fatigues. He walked with a confidence in his steps and the aura of the true soldier that he was, unafraid to face adversity to reach his goal. He motioned everyone nearby to gather around him. Danny could hear a pin drop while the men involved in the rescue effort waited impatiently for what the councilman had to say.

Standing in front of his men and support staff, Councilman Arevalo locked eyes with everyone one by one and said, "You all know we're gathered here today to get a foreign hostage back. But most importantly, we are going to purge Commander Berto and his army of bandits from these islands. It's time to finally take our island back from those lawless criminals and bring back the days when our people roamed these seas without fear of being kidnapped or harmed. When we meet with Commander Berto and his men, he will want to see Danny demonstrate his experiment to show it works. After that, Helen will make the wire transfer through a satellite phone. As soon as the money clears, the hostage will be transferred to one of our boats. The boat driver will immediately drive away in a zigzag pattern to clear the area and bring Danny, Helen and the hostage to safety. Following that, we will open fire on Commander Berto and his men to eliminate them all for good!" Arevalo said.

The men waved their rifles in the air, hooting and hollering and mimicking the sounds of a battle drum. Danny stole a glance at Helen. All he had ever wanted to do was to get Blake back. Now he and Helen were involved in an island squabble and a military operation to kill a known terrorist. He feared that the councilman's daring plan was too risky. The chance of stray bullets hitting Helen, Blake or himself was too great. He took a step forward wanting to reason with the councilman not to follow such a dangerous strategy. But as he got closer to the councilman, the men's chanting grew louder. The die is cast. Anything could go wrong, but he felt powerless to stop the plan in motion. There was nothing else to do but to cross the Rubicon and head into the heart of Sulu Sea.

The bloodthirsty men wanted to see the Kulog ng Timog's blood staining the blue sea.

"What if Commander Berto and his men out maneuver us and escape?" Vic shouted over the men's hooting.

"We've already thought of that scenario. Anyone who slips off the barrage of bullets we're about to unload will be met by Lieutenant Dimagiba's fast-attack patrol boat with its armor-piercing machine guns and who will be tracking the progress of our mission," Arevalo answered, pointing to the military officer standing next to him.

"Let's go!" Vic shouted.

Danny and Helen followed the councilman and his bodyguards to the five speedboats waiting on the beach. Danny hopped on the green boat where five men with machine guns and M-14s in their hands and ammunition belts around their waist were already seated.

Careful to not damage the already fragile coral reef and to avoid puncturing the hull's bottom, the drivers slowly pushed the boats out to the open sea with a long pole. As soon as the boats cleared the shallow water, the drivers simultaneously pulled their starter ropes. The sound of the engines' pistons simultaneously rumbling roused everyone in the vicinity. Even the birds on the beach searching for fish scattered from the loud booming engines.

Reaching the open water, the drivers turned the boats away from Bongao on predetermined GPS waypoints and opened up the throttle. The ten-foot speedboats and their massive outboard engines roared like angry lions, vibrating the passengers. The boat pitched up as it glided across the turquoise sea. The shoreline quickly receded. They passed by small fishing boats lowering their nets into the water. Danny grasped the boat's sides to keep from sliding. He puckered his lips as the salty sea splashed in his face. Helen squinted as the wind blew hard into her eyes. Steadily, the boat's speed inched faster until reaching close to 35 knots. As they gained more distance, the sight of Bongao shrank on the horizon like a straw hat floating away.

SWELLS OF RISING WAVES appeared out of nowhere. The speedboat jumped off the crest of a two-foot wave and went airborne for a few seconds. Danny felt a sudden lightness at the bottom of his stomach from the abrupt weightlessness. He felt himself falling into an abyss. Suddenly, the boat slammed back onto the flat surface of the sea. The boat's momentum shoved Danny and Helen forward. Danny quickly grabbed the railing to prevent from being thrown overboard. He checked to see how Helen was coping with the brain-jarring ride. He reached for her hand to comfort her. She responded with a tight squeeze and did not let go. As they navigated through the expansive Sulu Sea toward their mysterious destination, Danny wondered if he and Helen would ever find the meeting place in the middle of an unforgiving body of water.

After two and a half hours of hard driving, Popoy

Arevalo raised his hand and the drivers throttled back. The speedboats began to slow down and finally stopped. Danny and Helen were relieved to not be slamming into the waves, but almost immediately the boat began rolling from side to side. The motion was nauseating.

The councilman turned the handheld VHF radio on, pressed the push-to-talk button and transmitted a message on the predetermined frequency.

"Are we here?" Helen asked. Her voice sounded tired.

A choppy voice crackled. The councilman was speaking to the person on the other end in a regional dialect Danny could not understand except for the occasional Tagalog word.

"I think he was speaking to Commander Berto," Danny said, trying to piece it all together.

FROM A DISTANCE, three speedboats appeared on the horizon approaching them in a zig-zagging pattern.

"They're here! Commander Berto is the one with the red bandana around his head," the councilman said.

The VHF handheld radios flooded with chatter. Commander Berto went around them and made a circling gesture with his hand in the air to follow him. The boats' engines came back to life and for the next half-hour they followed Commander Berto and his ragtag band of fighters to lead them to yet another location.

Finally, the boats stopped. Commander Berto positioned his boats parallel to the councilman's armada and ordered him to inch closer. Once they were at spitting distance, the councilman gave Berto an adversarial stare.

Commander Berto stood no taller than five feet five inches, sporting a goatee and a pair of dark sunglasses. For an animal who had beheaded several hostages in the past, he looked like an average, brown-skinned fisherman.

For the first time since Blake had left San Diego more than two months ago, Danny saw his best friend again. He was instantly filled with relief that his friend was still alive and well. Blake was wearing a white T-shirt that was torn on the sides and a pair of shorts that didn't seem to fit. Danny checked Blake's exposed arms and legs for any signs of bruising or trauma, but he was glad to see that his skin bore no marks of physical abuse.

"We're gonna get you out of here soon, Blake," Helen said.

"I need to see the money and the compound," Commander Berto shouted in a mocking tone.

Helen opened the knapsack and pulled out the clear plastic bag containing a hundred thousand dollars. Commander Berto cracked a menacing grin.

"Toss it over here," he shouted.

Helen complied.

"Here's the Cube," Danny said as he opened the luggage.

"I want everyone off the boat except you two," Commander Berto said, pointing to Danny and Helen.

"You heard him," Arevalo barked. His armed

bodyguards quickly complied and transferred to the other boats while Danny and Helen remained.

"Take this and get Blake in here," Danny said, pointing to the open rollaway exposing the Rx-18 compound.

"We need to test what you've got and you better hope they work or your friend is finished," Commander Berto stated.

"Blake, we've never tested this in a warmer body of water. The mix is not for these parts of the world," Danny said.

"It's OK. We'll do it like we have done before," Blake replied. "We'll just use the sonar to detect the fish. I'll tell you when to drop the Cube in the water. Did you bring a sonar?"

Danny handed the handheld fish-finder to Blake, along with the sensor attached to the 25-foot wire.

"Move away from us," Commander Berto ordered the councilman and his men.

Blake placed the portable sonar's sensor in the water and checked the screen. He moved the sensor left and then right looking for some fish activity. Spotting a school of fish circling below the boats, he signaled Commander Berto to move closer. Commander Berto followed Blake's directions and slowly, at almost an idle speed, he carefully moved the boat so as to not disturb the unidentified sea life below them. Danny gently pushed the throttle forward and followed Blake's lead.

Blake saw an increase of dots on the screen, indicating

that the scanner had picked up a school of fish in the area. Realizing that he was right above a school of fish, he shouted, "Drop the cube now!"

Danny tore open the sealed plastic bag and threw a book-sized portion of the Rx-18 compound in the water.

No one knew what Danny and Blake were trying to achieve. Even Helen looked confused. After so many years of research and so many failed tests, Danny wondered if the compound would actually work, not just to attract the fish but also to finally end Blake's nightmare.

Danny waited, barely able to contain his emotions. Twenty minutes passed. It felt like a lifetime as everyone exchanged glances and held their breath. As they searched below, it became clear that not only were the large groups of fish not attracted by the Cube's properties, they actually seemed propelled to scatter away. It was the same disheartening result Danny and Blake had seen in so many of their previous experiments. The situation grew even tenser as Commander Berto began stroking the AK-47 resting on his lap. Danny knew that if Commander Berto wasn't convinced that his invention would work, it would mean Blake's demise.

"Looks like you two are just stalling for time," Commander Berto said. "If I don't see some results—and quickly—I hate to think what I'll have to do. I promise none of you will like it."

Desperate for a solution, Danny called to Blake, "Give me the fish finder and I'll search for the fish. Be ready to drop another cube on my signal." Danny threw a pack of Rx-18 compound in Blake's boat.

Helen took the helm and slowly steered the boat while Danny gave her directions. After another tension-filled five minutes, Danny finally saw a school of fish gathering near the front of the boat. He raised his hand and made a cutting gesture across his throat, instructing everyone to turn their engines off so that the fish wouldn't get spooked and swim away.

Blake threw the Cube several feet away from the boat into the sea. Immediately, fish started swimming toward it with another group approaching in the periphery. Estimating the next school's distance, Danny asked Blake to throw several more of the Rx-18 compound around them.

Suddenly, fish after fish came up to the surface. Danny looked at Blake who had a look of pained relief painted on his face. In the middle where the boats formed a circle, different varieties of fish began to appear. Danny watched the backs of the fish just below the surface of the metallic blue water. Ten, twenty, fifty, and then hundreds of fish began jumping and crowding in circle between the boats. Danny felt a twinge of joy and a bit of pride at the sight of so many different varieties of fish attracted to the Rx-18 compound. He almost began to relax knowing that he was closer to bringing Blake home.

Commander Berto waved his hand and signaled for Danny's boat to come forward. Helen nudged the throttle and moved closer to Commander Berto.

"Now that you have proof that the Rx-18 compound works, can I have my friend back?"

"Not so fast, cowboy," Commander Berto said. "Not until I have confirmation that the rest of my money has been transferred."

Helen took out the digital pad to scan her fingers and confirm her identity.

"Looks like today is going to be a good day for me," Commander Berto said with a self-satisfied look.

"Who paid you to get the compound from us?" Danny asked.

Commander Berto contemplated the question for a moment, mulling over if he wanted Danny to know the truth to his query.

"Since I don't really care, let's just say that a certain fishing company is very interested in your invention. I'm going to make a fortune off of your hard work—two million euros to be exact, plus the million dollar bonus you brought me. And if you see Dr. Klein, that Yankee Doodle Dandy, action-hero wannabe, tell him that I got the big payday today and not to bother contacting me. Our business relationship is over."

Commander Berto retrieved the satellite phone from his bag. He was about to turn it on when the rumbling of an approaching boat caught their attention. Danny looked to his left and saw a grey-colored Navy patrol boat approaching at a very high speed. Danny felt his knees weakening, distraught from the patrol boat's horrendous timing.

"What the fuck is this?" Commander Berto shouted, thrusting the throttle all the way forward causing the engines to howl in thunderous anger as he steered his craft toward the sun with Blake still on board.

As Commander Berto's boat lurched forward, Blake lost his balance and fell to his knees. In the split second before the speedboat disappeared from sight, Blake looked back. He looked terrified as he lost sight of his friends, an expression of crushing disappointment cascading down his face. This was to be a day of celebration and reunion, as Blake was going to be finally freed from his captors. As the expanse of water grew between their boats, hope of ever seeing Blake freed from his captivity seemed lost.

Commander Berto's men in the two Kulog ng Timog speedboats began spraying bullets towards the councilman's party and the approaching Navy patrol boat. The councilman and his men seemed unable to react to the quickly changing situation. Most of his men's rifles weren't cocked and ready for action. They couldn't react fast enough to return fire. One of the councilman's speedboat hulls was pierced by several rounds of bullets and almost immediately tumbled to one side. Fearing that his men would drown, he maneuvered his boat to rescue his men. Finding an opportunity to escape, one of the Kulog ng Timog's boats sprinted away. The approaching patrol boat made a quick turn and pursued the fleeing speedboats driven by Commander Berto and his men. The other speedboat floored it and headed into the open sea. Arevalo ordered one of his speedboats to chase after Kulog ng Timog while he pulled out his men from the paralyzed speedboat, taking in more and more water with each passing second.

STUNNED BY THE SUDDEN TURN of events and not wanting to lose Blake, Danny quickly got behind the wheel and chased after him. He gripped the steering wheel hard, holding on for dear life. Danny's boat zoomed across the ocean with incredible speed, but it was still too slow to catch up with Blake's boat. Danny squinted his eyes but all he could see was the outline of Blake's body getting smaller and smaller until it was just a dot between the sea and sky.

"Is there anyone behind us?" Danny shouted over the deafening engine and wind noise.

Helen turned and scanned the horizon. "I don't see anyone."

Danny desperately searched the sapphire surface of the sea for any sign of where Blake might be. Their situation looked bleak. His only option was to follow the trail of aluminum lather that Commander Berto's boat left behind, hoping it would lead him to where Blake was being taken.

Danny maintained the same course, but after an hour into the chase, the trail they were following was swallowed by the waves. It became impossible to know which direction Commander Berto went.

"See anything?" Danny asked.

Helen shielded her eyes with her hand from the harsh sun, desperately looking for anything that was moving on the skin of the grey water.

"I don't see anything."

He had no choice but to face the fact that Commander Berto had vanished into the vast expanse of the Sulu Sea with Blake. He turned his attention back to the boat, realizing they would soon run out of gas. If that happened, they would be dead on the water.

"Where are we?" Helen asked.

Danny checked the GPS. "We're about one hundred and fifty miles from Bongao."

Danny lifted a five-gallon plastic jug from the back of the boat. He shook it but didn't hear any gas sloshing inside.

"Fuck," Danny said, seeing a bullet hole at the bottom of the gas can.

He unscrewed the gas cap on the motor's tank, but it was hard to tell how much was still left. He searched around the floor and found a stick. He dipped it in the gas tank praying that there was plenty left. As he lifted it out, he saw the tip of the stick was only an inch wet.

"I don't think we could make it back. Looks like we have just over a gallon of gas left," Danny said, securing the cap back on.

Helen lifted the seat covers and searched through the compartments underneath anticipating extra gas cans. Instead, she found a handheld VHF radio. She turned it on and static crackled.

"Councilman Arevalo…can you hear us? This is Danny and Helen."

"Stop it, Helen!" Danny yelled.

"I have to do something or the sharks will have us for dinner."

"All you're doing is transmitting our location. Dr. Klein could be listening and triangulating our exact spot. You're going to get us killed."

"Shit," she said, dropping the radio on the floor. "Those damn bandits are going to kill him!"

Devastated at missing the opportunity to get Blake back, she sat on the bench and buried her head in her lap. They faced the possibility of floating in the middle of the Sulu Sea for days, if not weeks, without food or water. Danny moved near her and held her close to his chest, trying to comfort her in their dire situation.

"He won't do that. He's a greedy bastard and he wants the big payday."

Danny checked the sun's direction and saw that it was already a quarter way down the sky. With each passing minute, the daylight's strength was subsided. It would be extremely dangerous to float in the water at night. Danny racked his brain for a way to escape their sticky situation. There was nothing but the swells of the unforgiving sea.

He surveyed the vast expanse of water and wondered if he could get to a small island for safety. Checking the time, he saw it was 2:00 p.m. He rotated the dial on his wristwatch, pointing the arrow toward the sun's direction.

"We need to get to an island," he said.

"I see nothing but water," Helen remarked with exasperation.

He showed her a map of the Philippines on his phone. Sliding his thumb and the tip of his forefinger, he expanded the area only covered by the Sulu Sea. Unfortunately, only the larger islands showed and the distances were too far for them to reach.

"We're somewhere between Tawi-Tawi and Palawan. Our best bet is to get to Mapun Island, but I don't think we have enough gas to get there."

"What do we do next?"

"I don't know how far the remaining gas would take us. I think it would be better if we just drift with the current until we see a small island. As soon as we spot one, we'll use the remaining gas to take us there."

Exhausted and disheartened by the series of nonstop disasters, Danny pressed his back to the side of the boat and remained quiet as they waited for the sea to take them to safety.

AFTER DRIFTING FOR HOURS, Helen couldn't believe her eyes when she saw a clump of coconut trees blooming on a mound of white sand. At first, she thought she was hallucinating from thirst and from the nearly two-hour sun exposure.

"Island! Over there," Helen shouted, pointing to the atoll directly in front of them.

Danny was elated by the thought of finally setting foot on terra firma. Danny and Helen hugged each other, joyous, if only briefly, knowing they'd be safe from the sharks lurking near their boat.

Danny rushed to the outboard motor and yanked the starter rope with one hard pull. The engine woke up from its slumber, growling in excitement. He pointed the boat towards the tiny atoll. Slowly, the tiny speck of land grew larger and larger into view.

JUST AS THEY WERE ABOUT to reach the atoll, the engine began to sputter like it was on its dying breath. Danny shot a glance at Helen. The fear in her eyes was palpable.

"What's going on?"

He visually inspected the engine hoping to find a minor problem. His hopes were crushed when he saw a sticky trail of gas oozing from a bullet hole on the side of the gas tank.

"You stupid boat..." Danny cursed under his breath.

Starved of fuel, the engine died. They began drifting to the side. All Danny and Helen could do was to watch their atoll of salvation move farther away.

Not wanting to just give up, Helen lifted the seat covers

to find a folded, military style shovel and a pair of old flippers. They began paddling toward the island. While they propelled the boat forward, the current was too strong and kept pulling them away from safety. Seeing that their situation was deteriorating by the minute, Danny donned the pair of flippers, jumped in the water and began pushing the boat toward the island. He kicked as hard as he can, Helen paddling with the same determination. Danny synchronized his kicks with her strokes to maximize their efficiency.

After an agonizing hour, Danny finally felt the tip of his toes touch the white sand. The atoll was no bigger than an average-sized concert stadium. Danny looked down the transparent absinthe green water and saw his feet digging into the sand. Helen grabbed the long pole from the floor and pushed the boat forward.

Their hard work finally paid off when Danny heard the sweet sound of the hull's bottom scraping on the sand.

Drained of all their energy, they collapsed on the beach. Helen reached for Danny's hand, thankful for his gallant efforts to save them.

She looked up and saw the lemon sun shining brightly, coconut trees bowing low in the wind.

THEIR THIRST AND HUNGER eventually caught up to them. Danny looked through the boat's compartment, hopeful he'd discover a water container and some fruit to eat. Instead, he found a folded plastic sheet, a green duffel bag, a flashlight, and a bolo knife.

"Is there any water?"

Danny emptied the duffel bag's contents on the sand and found a book of matches, a bag of rice, a small cooking pot, several cans of corned beef, some plastic cups, and a bottle of lambanog.

"What are we going to drink?" Helen asked. "I'm really thirsty."

"Coconut juice," Danny replied.

With the bolo in his hand, Danny cut a wedge off the trunk of the coconut tree and used it to get up the tree—cutting more wedges as he ascended.

"Back off," Danny shouted from the top of the tree.

He sliced the stems, coconuts falling one by one onto the sand.

"Think we have enough?" Helen asked, surveying the twenty gourds on the ground.

Holding the bolo firmly, Danny began chopping the husk off a coconut until exposing the shell. With its point, he cut a small hole.

"This is so good and refreshing," Helen said, drinking the clear juice.

After Danny and Helen finished their drink, he cut the coconut in half, exposing its semitransparent meat. Helen was about to scoop the meat from the shell with her fingernails when Danny stopped her.

"Wait, I want to show you this."

He cut away a piece of fresh husk and formed it into the

shape of a shoehorn.

"And?" Helen asked.

"Use it to scrape the meat off the shell," Danny said, handing it to her.

WHILE SHE ENJOYED the coconut meat, Danny reached into his knapsack and pulled out the VHF radio. He pressed the scan button and listened for random radio transmissions but heard only white noise. He switched the channel to the international distress frequency and sent out an SOS. He clicked the push-to-talk switch—three quick bursts, three long bursts, then another three quick bursts—repeating the process several times. A few minutes later, he made a mayday call, announcing their GPS coordinates in hope that the Coast Guard could hear his message or triangulate his signal.

With the sky turning yellow and night fast approaching, Danny and Helen worked to build a shelter. They ventured further inside the atoll to gather dried sticks and coconut leaves. Danny dug holes in the sand, burying a quarter of a long stick and forming an A-frame for a makeshift tent. Helen tied the coconut leaves to the sides and fashioned them into walls.

"Our palace in the sand is not too bad," Danny said, looking at his first architectural accomplishment.

"I'll order furniture online. Do you think they'll be here tomorrow?" Helen asked with playfulness in her voice.

"Don't forget the string lights I'll want to hang from

that tree to the top of our house. Then I'll put the dining table right over there," Danny said, pointing to an open space near a short coconut tree, "so we can dine under the stars."

"We could have had a real dining set and a real bedroom with a bedspread and ten matching pillows," Helen replied, picking up loose leaves around the tent while avoiding his eyes.

Danny was taken aback by her comment. He thought that he was the only one who had regrets about their breakup years ago. He wanted to be open and honest and to tell her that their breakup wasn't entirely his fault. She was equally to blame. Not wanting to get into an argument, he pretended not to grasp her comment's undertone.

"It's dinner time," Danny said, digging through the duffel bag.

Realizing that she was out of line for starting the blame game, she quickly changed her demeanor. "I think we're having steak for dinner."

"There you go!" Danny said, retrieving the can of corned beef.

"Now all we need is a bottle of Worcestershire sauce and we're set."

"Oh, I almost forgot—we have coconut wine," Danny said.

"And for our evening's entertainment..." Helen said, pressing the play button on her phone. A love song filled the quiet night.

Danny took a sip of the lambanog and passed it to Helen.

THE SUN DIPPED below the horizon, its orange rays reflecting on the underside of the clouds. The sky turned into a canvass, painted with smudges of orange and dark pink.

Danny dug a hole in the sand, filling it with dried branches and leaves. Lighting it with a match, the flame from the bonfire radiated warmth and comfort at the same time. They found the pulsating amber light soothing.

"What if we never get off of this island?" Helen asked.

"It will be many long nights spent in front of the fire with a diet of freshly-caught fish and coconut juice."

"That wouldn't be too bad."

"I can take up residence on the other side of the atoll just in case you get tired of seeing me every day."

"I prefer that you're just a few feet away from me," Helen said.

The embers flew in erratic patterns and died off as they blended into the still air. Though Danny didn't know when a rescue boat would ever pass by, in a strange way he was glad because he was spending the night alone with Helen.

"I am sorry for disappearing from your life. I had to stay away from you because you told me that being a teacher meant so much to you. I knew that if I asked you to stay with me in San Diego, you would have stayed but given up on your dreams. I didn't want you to resent me."

"That was for me to decide and not you. I'm big girl. I can handle the consequences of the choices I make. All those years we were apart, I kept asking myself what I had done wrong."

"You didn't do anything wrong. There's not a day that goes by when I don't think about the stupidest mistake I've made in my life—not telling you what was on my mind. I could have at least flown out to see you every three months or so," Danny said.

"You knew where I was. How come you never visited?" Her face contorted into perplexity.

"Leaving you was the biggest mistake I ever made in my life. I thought of you often, especially those lonely nights in my apartment. I'm really sorry for all the years I've been excessively proud. I should've dropped whatever I was doing, gone to Boston, and begged you to come back to me. I could have taken a teaching position at the local university and still done my research on the side."

"Not moving back to San Diego to be close to you wasn't the best decision I ever made either," Helen said. "What are we going to do when this whole thing is over and we're back in San Diego?"

He reached for a piece of her hair dangling on the side of her face and tucked it behind her ear. It was soft on his fingertips. He had dreamt of the day when they would finally be reunited. She stared at him with her sparkling blue-grey eyes. Guided by his longing to make up for all the lost time, Danny moved toward her, kissing her pink lips. They were sweeter than any tree-ripened fruit on a hot summer day. The woman that he had always loved was back in his arms again.

"I've always loved you and I don't want to waste my days without you."

"Oh Danny," Helen responded, tears running down her cheeks.

Danny gently laid Helen on the soft sand. He slowly kissed the side of her neck up to the back of her ears, taking his time and savoring each kiss. Helen tensed her leg muscles and let out a soft moan. Reaching behind her, Danny unsnapped her bra, tenderly pushing her blouse above her head and exposing her breasts. She pressed the palms of her hands on his tight abs, ran them all the way up to his shoulders, and pulled his shirt off. They stared at each other full of longing and desire to let their hands freely explore each other's naked bodies. Helen wrapped her arms around his neck and pulled him tight. Her breasts were soft as they pressed against his chest, tremors of ecstasy arcing across his spine.

They had waited for so long to be in each other's arms—there was no reason to rush. The moonlight painted their naked bodies.

Pressing his lips against hers, their tongues danced inside their mouths. A sense of lightness formed at the base of his stomach, electrified by his longing for her, and delighted his manhood. He pressed his face into her hair, inhaling her pure love. Elated with the medley of his touches, she spread her legs and pressed her hands into his shoulder blades.

"Oh Danny, I want you," Helen beseeched.

He slowly guided his being into her femininity.

Helen moaned with pleasure and Danny droned in ecstasy with each of his gentle thrusts. The rustling of the leaves and the rolling waves on the shore joined the echoes of their lovemaking.

Helen looked into the black sky as she climaxed. As Danny peaked, the jewel of stars reflecting in her eyes grabbed his consciousness. Within that vision, he knew he was finally home.

DANNY SAT IN THE SHADE, tying a pointed metal tip to the end of the pole he would devise into a harpoon. He couldn't believe that such a paradise could exist in the middle of the Sulu Sea while turmoil and lawlessness swirled around him. He looked up and saw Helen walking toward him with a handful of seashells she'd picked from the beach. A part of him wished that no one had heard yesterday's SOS transmission and that he and Helen would never be rescued. He could spend the rest of his life alone with her and never to return to the chaos of modern life. It was sad that it had taken the tragedy of Blake's abduction to realize that he wanted to spend the rest of his life with her.

"I gathered something to decorate our little house."

"You know in the old days, when a man wanted a woman to be his wife, the courtship tradition was to help with her family's household chores, fetching water from the well or chopping fire wood. It showed her family that he was capable of providing for her and to prove that his intentions to marry were serious."

Helen looked him straight in the eye and said, "Maybe you can start by catching some fish for brunch?" A sly smile broke out at the corners of her mouth.

"I guess I better get to work before the rush hour traffic," Danny said.

Anchoring the long rope to a tree, he pushed the speedboat further out into the sea. He sat on the edge of the boat and closed his eyes for a moment to determine how he would catch a fish. The light from the bright sky created a red dome against the back of his eyelids. He opened his eyes and donned a pair of flippers and a diving mask. He looked down at the transparent evergreen water and then jumped into the shallow reef.

He held his breath as he dove deeper into the water. Floating over the coral reef, he marveled at the miracle of nature. He felt one with the sea. Stacks of flat, disk-like fans competed for the sunlight penetrating the water. Pink, purple and lime-green fingers seemed to be reaching toward the surface, mocha-brown cauliflower formations surrounding him.

Seeing some spiny lobsters crawling on the seabed, he

grabbed them by their backs. He surfaced, throwing the lobsters onto the boat, and then dove back down. He harpooned a silver fish with transparent fins and yellow and blue stripes along its sides. Satisfied with his catch, he rowed the boat back to the beach.

Danny couldn't believe his eyes when he got back to their makeshift tent. Helen was waiting for him with the fire already going in the shallow pit and a rice pot over the flame. Next to her was a low table covered with banana leaves. Danny was impressed with her domesticity.

"The table was delivered overnight after all," Helen said.

"I'm impressed with your handiwork, Ms. Glass," Danny said, placing his catch on the table. "On the menu today, we have grilled lobster, barbecued fish and squid."

"And for dessert, we'll have chocolate lava cake," Helen replied, placing a chocolate bar on the makeshift table.

WITH STOMACHS FULL and satisfied souls, the newly-reunited couple walked along the beach. The sun was hot against their skin, but the blowing wind cool on their faces. It felt good walking together holding hands. The sand felt like stepping on pure sugar.

"This place is so beautiful. It's like our own private island," Helen said, wrapping her arms above his waist.

"Maybe this whole tragedy happened so that you and I can be together again," Danny said, pulling her closer.

"What are you planning to do to get us out of here?"

Danny contemplated what to tell her. He had a couple of options: to keep sending mayday messages in hope that the Coast Guard would detect their distress calls or, if things got desperate, load the boat with food and water and set out in the open sea and pray that a passing ship might discover them. Not knowing what to tell her, he looked down and watched tiny crabs with periscope eyes dashing sideways toward a hole in the sand.

"Danny! What's that floating on the horizon?" Helen asked, tugging his arm excitedly.

He squinted his eyes against the glare reflecting off the water. He saw what looked like a shark's dorsal fin jutting across the surface. Then he realized it was a fishing boat's tall mast with lines running down from the top. The answer to his dilemma had just been found.

"Quick! We need to signal the boat to come get us," Danny said, running to their makeshift tent. "Get your compact mirror!"

She opened her handbag, pulled out her compact mirror, and aimed it at the fishing boat hoping to signal for help. Not wanting to waste another precious second, Danny lit the dried leaves, branches and twigs he had prepared earlier in anticipation of a passing boat. White smoke billowed against the blue sky. Danny ran into the water. Ankle deep, he waved his arms and shouted, "Over here! Help!"

AS IF KING NEPTUNE himself heard their cries

for help, the fishing boat began turning toward them, bobbing with the waves.

"We're finally being rescued!" Helen shouted elatedly, hugging Danny.

It was the most beautiful thing Danny had ever seen. The large fishing boat's outrigger arms stretched out to embrace them.

As soon as the boat's bow scraped the sand, its fishermen dropped the ramp to dismount. A dark-skinned man in a faded orange shirt and denim shorts with tattered ends stepped down, introducing himself as Captain Roger.

He was a thin man, but looked strong from his stance. As soon as he smiled, a set of yellow teeth showed through his stretched lips. Bewilderment painted on his face, he studied the two strange-looking characters—an American woman wearing nothing but an oversized T-shirt and a muscular Filipino man who seemed to be out of place.

"How did you get here? By that boat?"

"We were going to the Turtle Islands to research its creatures, but we got stranded here," Helen quickly lied.

"That's far from here," Roger said.

"Sir, can you take us back to Tawi-Tawi?" Danny asked.

"That's about a hundred fifty miles away. Besides, we're going the opposite direction. We're on our way to go fishing tonight, and after that we're heading straight to Palawan to sell our catch. I could radio the Coast Guard for help when we get to Palawan and tell them to get you.

Maybe they'll come tomorrow."

Danny thought about the risk of calling out on unsecured radio frequencies. He was confident that Dr. Klein was already aware of what had happened yesterday and could already be listening to all radio chatter.

"We need to get off the island now. Can you help us, please?" Helen said.

"Even if I'd like to take you with us, we can't handle the added weight."

"Take this is for your troubles," Danny pleaded, showing Roger a fistful of hundred dollar bills. "Please take us with you. This should cover the fish weight you'll lose from tonight's catch."

THE MURMUR OF WAVES splashing on the shore kept Danny and Helen calm throughout their solitary stay on the tiny island, but the pinging sounds of an eight-cylinder motor back at work was music to their ears. They sat in the middle of the boat and watched the atoll they had called home for the last two days fade in the distance. The last time Danny saw the atoll from the same perspective, his pulse had been going at hundred miles per hour as he wondered if they'd live another day.

The fishermen balanced themselves on the beams as they walked back and forth fixing the lines and preparing the nets. White foam formed at the tips of the sea. Suddenly, a group of dolphins appeared.

"Look, over there!" Helen said excitedly, pointing

several yards away.

The dolphins arched their backs and jumped out the surface of the water. More agile than the fishing boat, they playfully swam next to it while keeping speed with the boat. Looking at them, Danny remembered that they were one of the major reasons why he fell in love with the ocean. They moved closer to the side of the fishing boat. The dolphins' shapes were visible just a few inches below the surface. Then with one fluid move, they jumped up toward the bow as if daring the boat to run them over.

IT WAS PAST MIDNIGHT when they reached the fertile grounds to hunt for their prized tunas. Stars twinkled like solitaires around the faint moon. Roger ordered his crew to cut the engine and prepare the fishing nets. Almost immediately, the fishing boat began to undulate with the waves' up and down motion.

"Do you have a high powered, two-way radio with auto-patch capability so I could make a phone call?" Danny asked.

"I have one but we won't be able to reach the repeater till we're about five miles from Palawan Island. I usually use it to alert my buyers right before we arrive to tell them how much fish we've caught."

The crew hit the lights and pointed them down into the water.

"What's that for?" Helen asked.

"They're trying to draw in the fish," Danny answered.

One of the crew members dropped the end of the fishnet with a marker buoy on the end. Roger guided the fishing boat in a circular pattern. After making a complete circle, Roger ordered his men to tie the bottom of the fishnet and pull it up. When the fishnet was hoisted back up, the result was disappointing. The net was barely full, with mostly small fish that wouldn't command a high-market price.

"Is that an effective way to catch fish?" Danny asked.

"Most of the time, yes, but the bright light also invites all kinds of fish. Mostly the ones I don't care for. We're not lucky on this spot. I have to go to a different location," Roger replied, signaling his crew to move on.

"How do you know where to shine the light where most of the fish are?" Danny asked, trying to change the subject.

"I use a fish radar, but every time I get near a school they scatter."

Danny inspected the incandescent light bulbs used to shine the light on the water. He flicked them on and off and noticed that the lights were too bright.

"I think that while the tiny fish are attracted to the light, the approaching fish are blinded by it too, and that's why they disperse. It's like attracting a moth. As soon as it feels the heat, it flies away. We need to tone it down. Do you have any green plastic sheets?"

When Roger and one of his assistants returned, they brought a handful of green plastic bags. Danny placed the green bags under different lights.

"Now turn on the lights," Danny said.

Roger observed the activity on the sonar's monitor screen and steered the boat into the area with the highest fish density.

"Drop the net."

Danny broke a piece of the Cube, placed it inside a small bag with a weight inside and tied it to the end of a 20-foot rope. He watched the sonar's console indicating where the school of fish was swimming. The way they moved was tricky. It was as if they were dancing in the ocean and not following a particular pattern. Danny had been in the same situation before when he conducted his research. Detecting the school of fish was easy, but the fish usually swam away.

Danny retrieved a light stick from his knapsack and tossed it in the water. "Turn the lights off, then decrease speed."

Roger reached for the throttle and powered down. Danny threw another chunk of the Cube in front of him. Roger's eyes lit up when he saw that the fish had not scattered. As if the stars revealed the serendipitous moment, Danny realized the mistake he had been making. There was nothing wrong with the Rx-18 compound. It was ineffective because it wasn't being used properly. He had to conduct his experiments at night.

After the boat made a full circle, the net was slowly lifted. There were at least ten five-foot-long tunas caught.

"What did you throw in the ocean?" Roger asked. His

voice beamed with delight.

Eight

THE LONG ISLAND OF PALAWAN jutted out of the sea—the biggest island situated south of Luzon and west of the Visayas. Directly in front of the fishing boat, the mountain range stretched across like a wall, covered in its tea green carpet of lush trees. Danny took a deep breath and tasted the fresh, salty sea air on his lips. The morning sun was slowly pushing its way up into the fresh clear sky and the new day's rays were warming his face. He turned his cell phone on and was glad to see that there was a signal. Immediately, he dialed Melchor's number.

"Where are you? I've been worried sick."

"We're fine and about two hours away from Palawan. And you?"

"I'm confined in a hospital here in Manila. The doctors won't release me as a precaution until they are sure I am free from infections."

"What happened to you back in Jolo?"

"You wouldn't believe this but after several diagnostic tests, the doctors found that I had had a gallbladder attack. Couldn't be worse timing for my gallbladder to burst than while being chased by mercenaries, right?"

"You're right about that," Danny said.

"I was rushed to the operating room and the doctors took it out."

"I'm so pissed that our rendezvous with Kulog ng Timog got all screwed up. I thought we'd never get back."

"You must get to Puerto Princesa airport immediately and I'll send the plane to fly you to Manila. I'm on heavy pain medications and due for the next dose. I'll text you Commander Berto's go-between's number. Can you introduce yourself and see if there's something you can do?"

THE FISHING BOAT had anchored at the town of Narra. Rows of coconut trees lined the beach like rows of soldiers defending the island. As Danny jumped onto the fine textured sand, he was glad that he and Helen were back in civilization.

"Where do we go from here?" Danny asked, turning back to Roger.

"Keep going that way," Roger said, pointing in the direction of a trail leading to a dirt road. "You'll see people waiting on the side of the road for a bus going to Puerto Princesa, next to a sari-sari store."

"Thank you very much for the ride," Helen said.

Roger smiled at them and said nothing. Just as Danny was about to disappear into the thick vegetation, he turned back and waved goodbye to Roger, grateful that he had not left them for dead on the atoll.

WHEN DANNY AND HELEN arrived, the red, white and blue bus was being loaded up with goods, and the passengers were already lined up to get on board at the side of the road. Some of the passengers were climbing on the roof to find a seat between sacks of rice in brown burlap bags.

"We're not going to sit on the roof, are we?" Helen asked.

"Hope not," Danny replied, hurrying to the bus.

They carefully muscled their way through the passengers crowding the aisle. Swiveling his neck left and right in hope of an empty spot, he felt Helen tap his shoulder and point to a seat in the back with enough space for two people. Thrilled with her find, Danny turned his body sideways and squeezed himself between two men putting their belongings on the overhead racks. Breathing a sigh of relief, he extended his knees in the aisle and put his arm around Helen.

"I need a drink and something to eat," Helen said, pointing to the adolescent vendors carrying baskets of hard-boiled eggs, pork rinds, boiled peanuts and corn on the cob. Danny waved to a boy lugging a cooler. The kid pulled out an ice-cold soda, popped off the cap, and poured it into a clear plastic bag with a straw.

"I've never been served soda in a plastic bag," Helen said.

"That's because bottles here are treated like gold."

The driver started the engine and switched gears the second the bus was full. Almost immediately, the nauseating smell of diesel fume drifted inside the passenger compartment. Passengers who were lucky enough to have found vacant spots were crammed in their seats. Lost in thought, they balanced themselves by holding onto the bar attached on the ceiling, staring out into space with tired expressions on their faces. Danny pulled out his phone and quickly texted a message to the number Melchor had given him. *"This is Danny. I have the Cube with me. Where can I meet you?"*

He slouched in his seat and hoped that Commander Berto would soon receive his urgent request. Soon they were flying down the dirt road, a trail of dust billowing behind them.

AFTER A GRUELING HOUR of traveling in the crowded bus, Danny was glad when they arrived at the city of Puerto Princesa. They followed the passengers, eager to get off. As he was extending the handle on the rollaway to pull it behind him, he felt his phone vibrate in his pocket. He quickly checked it, glad to see it was a message from the go-between's number. *"Meet me in Cebu City. No police."*

"Read this," Danny said, showing his phone to Helen.

"We better get going."

"I'll tell the pilot to take us there right away when we see him."

While it was a relief to see so many tourists from around the world loitering around the Puerto Princesa Airport, excited to get on with their vacations to the white sands of El Nido and the crystal-clear waters of Coron—Australians, Japanese, Koreans, Germans, Canadians, Americans and locals from Manila—Danny felt a sense of melancholy. As Danny walked through the airport, he couldn't help but think he shouldn't be here, but instead be walking out of the San Diego International Airport with Blake beside him. He pictured the balloons and big signs that would be waiting at the terminal from friends and co-workers, welcoming Blake home with open arms. Instead, days had already gone by since the crisis began and Blake's rescue was still nowhere to be seen on the horizon. The burden of making contact with Kulog ng Timog hung heavy over his head.

The chartered airplane was already waiting when Danny and Helen walked out onto the tarmac. The same pilot who flew them to Jolo was standing outside with a worried look on his face.

"I'm glad you made it out without getting hurt," he said, assisting Helen up the stairs.

"It was a close call," Helen said, entering the cabin.

"Change of plans. We're going to Cebu City," Danny said, climbing onboard.

As soon as their belongings were secured, the two pilots wasted no time taxing onto the runway and passing the parked, wide-bodied jets. Without further ado, their plane took off, headed in Cebu City's direction.

Looking down from the window, Danny saw the tiny islands dotting the clear blue sea. He wondered if Blake was on one of them and looking up at the belly of the aircraft, helpless to get off and Danny helpless to pluck him out of his misery. It was strange to think how two people were in the same place at the same time yet their paths would never intersect.

About an hour and a half later, the pilot pointed the nose down, punched through the clouds, and then leveled the airplane's wings at around a thousand feet as it approached the central part of the island of Bohol. Danny and Helen looked out the window as the famous Chocolate Hills came into view. Covered with parched cocoa grass, they looked as if a giant had come in the middle of the night and poured lumps of brown rice across the flatland. The airplane flew closer to the ground. Danny could almost reach out the window and touch the treetops swaying with the wind. The parade of hills came into view and seemed to go on for miles. The plane banked toward Mactan-Cebu International Airport.

Nine

DANNY AND HELEN waited nervously at the base of the Magellan's Cross. Hexagonal with a red tile roof, the building housed a replica of the wooden cross erected by the Spaniards when they first landed in the country.

"How will the guide know that we're already here?" Helen asked.

"He's supposed to be here already and probably watching us to make sure that the police aren't with us," Danny replied.

The mural on the ceiling depicted scenes of the Spaniards planting a flag—their first encounter with the native people. A Spanish priest was busy converting the island's inhabitants to Christianity.

Danny imagined that momentous March day back in 1521 when Ferdinand Magellan, while searching for the Spice Islands, landed in the island nation and proved that the world wasn't flat after all. He wondered what it would have been like for his ancestors to see the sight of Magellan's fleet getting closer on the horizon, in their modern ships with their heavy firepower. Did they ever think that the paradise they were living in for thousands of years would be corrupted by the arrival of the Europeans? He thought of Magellan and his soldiers' demise. Though protected in their helmets and armor, their battle against *Lapu-Lapu,* the local chieftain, and his men was lost, defeated by only spears and long blades on the shallow beach. Though the native inhabitants' victory was sweet, enjoying its rewards was short lived. Several decades later, the Spanish came back with a vengeance. An armada with King Philip II's blessing—from which the country got its name—sent an expeditionary force with ships equipped with cannons and muskets all the way to Manila to divide and conquer the territory by siding with one tribe and defeating the other. The nation succumbed to the invaders, thus beginning what would be more than three hundred years of Spanish rule.

AN INCOMING TEXT message beep from Melchor interrupted Danny's trance. *"GET OUT OF THERE NOW! IT'S A TRAP!"*

The message sent tremors of fear throughout his brain. Realizing the immediate danger, he grabbed Helen by the arm.

"We need to go now!" Danny said, hurrying for the

exit.

A sudden jolt of panic shook Danny when he saw Dr. Klein standing just several feet away with two burly men. One of the men had curly hair and a massive body size, ominously smiling as he lifted his shirt to reveal his holstered gun. The other was bald with large muscular arms. The curly-haired man's large hand gripped his shoulder and the hard metal tip of a pistol pressed against his back.

"Don't run or we will shoot you and your girlfriend," Dr. Klein said, approaching the couple.

The bald man maneuvered behind Helen and wrapped his arm around her neck. She placed both hands on his arms and tried to wiggle away from his anaconda of an arm, but it was no use. Her thin slender arms were no match for his brute strength. Fearing he might meet his death on this island just like Magellan, Danny raised his hands up in the air.

"Okay, I give up. Please don't hurt her," Danny pleaded.

"Do you know how hard it was tracking your ass down?" Dr. Klein said.

"Did you hire that gang of kidnappers to get your hands on the Cube?" Danny asked.

"Now that you mention it, I wish I hadn't so I wouldn't have had to go through all this trouble. I just want the compound and then you'll never see me anymore. Capisce?"

"I need it to get Blake back."

"Do you think I give a damn about him? I don't care if he dies. Tell me where the compound is or I will order my men to party with your girlfriend before they kill her. So what's it gonna be, Einstein?"

Seeing that he had no other choice, Danny complied.

"Okay, okay. The compound is on the plane at the airport."

"See, it's not that hard to cooperate after all. Now here's the plan: We're going to the van that's waiting for us. Once we pick up the Cube, I promise I'll let you and your sweetie go," Dr. Klein said.

"How did you end up getting mixed up with a terrorist group?"

"Those motherfucking Kulog ng Timog hooligans are not the terrorists they claim to be. They're nothing but garden-variety, run-of-the-mill, everyday thugs for hire."

"Why were you trying to kill them?"

"That shit-face Commander Berto double-crossed me. I contacted that country bumpkin and proposed to kidnap Blake while conducting research in the Sulu Sea, giving him Blake's precise location and time of arrival. I need the Cube and that's why I concocted this ingenious plan to get it out of your lab. I figured if Blake was kidnapped and the ransom needed for his release was the Cube, you wouldn't hesitate to take it out from its secret location and bring it down here. Commander Berto was to pass it on to me and I was to pay him half a million dollars for his services, but the fucker got greedy. He contacted the NBH Fishing Industries—a Far East Asian company that owns several commercial fishing boats—and arranged to sell the Cube for half the price of what I had agreed to. Hell, he even had the audacity to demand an additional one million dollars in ransom from Blake's family. We had an agreement to lure you to an undisclosed beach on Basilan Island. It's only by dumb luck and through a network of paid informants that I found out his plans. That's when I realized that he had no intention of honoring our arrangement."

"Why do you want the Cube so bad? You know how to make one and you must have already realized by now that it does not work." Danny said.

"Not for your plans to save the world's fish population. When one of your lab assistants that I had carefully planted showed me a sample, I knew you were on to something good. You just didn't realize that your formula could also be used by the commercial fishing companies to catch more fish."

"That's the very reason why I invented the Cube! To stop the world's oceans from being depleted of its fish population.

"Enough of your idealistic view of the world. I want the Cube and I want my six million that I'll be paid for your invention. Now take me there."

WHILE PASSING BY a large crowd of people

gathered in the vicinity, Danny assessed the area around him searching for an escape. Dr. Klein was walking in front of them leading the group, followed by Helen and the bald man with his arm now around her waist. Danny was behind them with the curly haired man closely following him with the tip of the gun pointed to his spine. Even if he were able to run, Helen was still trapped in the bodyguard's vise-like grip. His eyes darted from side to side desperately looking for a way out for both of them.

He spotted a van that Dr. Klein had mentioned earlier parked on the street with the engine running. Just as they were about to pass a vendor stall, he made a swift pivot to the right, bent forward, grabbed the man's wrist, twisted it, and slammed the blade of his right hand on his captor's hand knocking the gun out. Danny followed up with a staccato of two quick, karate-style punches, landing hard blows to the man's throat and nose. The man fell down to his knees grasping his windpipe and struggling to breathe. The gun tumbled under a souvenir stall. He quickly searched for it but could not find it—precious seconds were being wasted. He did the second best thing and devised a weapon. Danny saw the three-foot sticks that served as the legs on the vendor's makeshift table on the sidewalk. He broke them off as its wooden toys and souvenirs crashed to the ground. Wanting to make sure that the curly-haired man was disabled, he whacked the man on the shoulders. The man rolled on the ground in agony.

Capitalizing on his momentum, Danny galloped at the man holding Helen. With a force equal to a Pacific Super Typhoon, Danny slammed the stick into the back of the man's head. Bright red blood painted his white collar. Subdued, the man inadvertently released Helen. Danny hooked the sticks around the man's neck and pulled him away from her.

"Helen, run!"

She sprinted into the crowd gathered around Magellan's Cross without looking back.

Danny threw the man down on the sidewalk and hit him again, this time on his thighs and torso. Seeing that the man couldn't move, Danny dropped the sticks and chased after Helen.

Dr. Klein turned around to assess what was going on. By the time he realized what had happened, Danny and Helen were gone.

"Get up! They're getting away," Dr. Klein shouted.

HELEN WAS ROUNDING the stall at full speed when she tripped on a crack in the concrete and fell. Luckily, Danny was closely following her. He quickly pulled her up by her armpits and helped her get up. "You okay?"

"I just banged my hip."

A series of deafening explosions reverberated in the air. Bullets tore through the sides of the buildings, tossing concrete splinters to the ground. Dr. Klein and his two hired guns sprinted in their direction. The terrified bystanders scattered in every direction, trying to get away from the flying bullets. With most of the people in the tourist area quickly thinning out, Danny worried that Dr. Klein and his men could easily spot them. Without the benefit of blending in with the sightseers, they would be easy prey. Helen joined the crowd as it dispersed. Danny was about to follow her but lost her in the mayhem. Out of the corner of his eye, he saw Helen sprinting in the harbor's direction.

After Danny had cleared the city center where Dr. Klein was shooting at them, he searched the buildings in the vicinity for Helen but couldn't find her. Careful not to be discovered, he squeezed his body into a nook on the side of the building and reached for his phone to call Helen. He was just dialing her number when his phone vibrated. Helen had sent him a text message. *"I'm in Fort San Pedro."*

DATING BACK to the late 1500s, Fort San Pedro is a triangular fortress built by the Spanish as protection against any faction, foreign or domestic, that might do the conquistadores harm. Danny hurriedly passed through the front entrance, pushing through tourists taking pictures along the manicured grounds. He worried that Dr. Klein or his men might have seen either one of them enter the stone fortress. If they did, then there was no escape.

Anxious to know where Helen was hiding, he texted,

"Where are you?"

His phone vibrated a few seconds later.

"I'm in one of the towers facing the street."

DANNY RAN ALONG the flagstone-covered pathway looking behind the bushes and along the walls. With all the sightseers roaming the grounds, it was difficult to find her. He was about to head toward the other end of the fortress when he heard Helen calling him.

"Danny!"

She ran to his arms and hugged him tight.

"I'm glad that you're okay," Danny said.

"How can we get back to the airport?"

"We can't go back that way," Danny said, pointing at the street below them. "Dr. Klein might be waiting for us."

"We need to get out of here. I think we can only exit through the main entrance."

Danny shifted his eyes to the ships and ferries that were passing by and said, "I think there is a way back to the airport without being recognized."

Careful not to be seen by Dr. Klein and his thugs, they quickly exited the stone fortress and pretended to be part of the Korean tourists anxious to get back onto their tour bus. Confident that the coast was clear, Danny and Helen sprinted along the shoreline and prayed that a ferry service was operating on time to get them safely to the island of Mactan where the airport was located.

HELEN WAS RELIEVED when she saw that the ferry headed for the island was still moored on the dock. She headed straight to the ticket booth and purchased their fares. Although the dock area was crowded with passengers waiting for their turn to get on the ferry, the boarding process ran smoothly. They walked down the ramp and stepped onto the boat. As soon as the last rope was disconnected from the pier, the ferry pulled away.

Helen leaned on his shoulder as tears began to roll down her cheeks. "We almost got captured."

He pulled her closer and hugged her tight to comfort her. Though Danny was glad that they had escaped a potential disaster, he knew that the odds were against them and it would only be a matter of time before Dr. Klein would catch up to them. Realizing that they weren't out of the woods yet, Danny called the pilot and said, "Please get the plane ready. We need to fly immediately."

THE MAJESTIC MAYON volcano came into view as the plane headed toward Manila over the southern part of the main island of Luzon. The massive mountain towering over the Bicol region was still active—and could erupt at any time. Looking out the window, Danny tried to make out the shape of a bell tower—the famous Cagsawa Ruins sticking out of the ground. The ruins were from an old church that was buried in lahar along with the rest of the town when the volcano erupted in the early 1800s. Danny worried that his chances of getting Blake back were sinking deeper into the abyss.

As the airplane flew further over Luzon, Danny saw patches of wasteland in the forest. The devastation was due to the *kaingin* system of farming—a slash-and-burn method that some of the farmers have been implementing throughout the years to clear out the thick vegetation for cultivation. With no tree roots to hold the topsoil intact, land erosion becomes inevitable when the heavy rain comes down each year.

He felt the airplane's nose dip. Danny looked out the window and saw the Taal Volcano's cratered tip protruding through Taal Lake. Somewhere in the far distance lay Manila, where they started their journey to make contact with Commander Berto. And now that journey was most likely to end as soon as they landed. With all possible avenues exhausted to get Blake back, and with Dr. Klein's relentless pursuit of the Cube, the only feasible plan was to notify the authorities of all that had happened and to ask for their help to rescue Blake. Danny knew he had to talk to Melchor to help the authorities negotiate with Kulog ng Timog now that the Cube had become a condition of Blake's release. He and Helen had tried their best but had been stopped or double-crossed at every turn. It was time to let the negotiators take charge and let fate decide the outcome.

As the airplane descended over Metro Manila and the pilot prepared to land, Danny looked down at the metropolis. The cityscape was inhabited by almost 12 million souls crammed into fashionable areas such as Makati, Las Piñas (famous for its bamboo organ), Parañaque, Navotas, Pateros (known for its duck eggs called *balut)*, Pasay, Taguig, Muntinlupa (renowned for its overcrowded prison), Marikina (popular for its selection of women's shoes), and Mandaluyong.

THE SMELL OF DISINFECTANT was overwhelming as Danny and Helen walked into the hospital. Relatives of confined patients were sitting along the hallway with worried looks on their faces. They entered a large room at the end of the hall where hospital beds were arranged side-by-side, giving no privacy to the patients. A nurse with a white cap pinned to her hair greeted them with a cordial smile.

"We're looking for Melchor Rodriguez," Danny said.

"There must be ten people by that name in this room alone. Check in at the registration desk, maybe someone might know," the nurse said, picking up a medical chart from the desk.

Melchor's private room was closed when they arrived. Danny knocked on the door and a female voice answered, asking them to wait as she finished changing his bandage.

A television game show blasting from a patient's room across the hallway caught his attention. The host in a multicolored suit was waving forty thousand pesos in the contestant's face—a woman in faded jeans and a pink t-shirt. The host asked her if she wanted to take the money and call it a day or pick the bag with a prize that could either be a brand new car or a toothpick. Her face contorted in confusion as she decided what to do. She turned to the crowd for answers but the frenzied shouting was just as confusing. Half of them were shouting to take the money and go home while the other half were shouting to pick the bag. She refused the money and pointed to the bag. The game show host added another twenty thousand pesos. She would have sixty thousand pesos if she decided to walk away with what equaled six month's salary for most workers. The host begged her to take the money but she was determined to win the mystery prize in the bag.

Danny compared her dilemma with how he should proceed with rescuing Blake. He thought of the contestant who was torn between walking away with the cash and her desire to push her luck and see what was in the bag. Maybe notifying the authorities would be good, but then again pressing on to find a way to get in contact with Kulog ng Timog would be better.

When Danny and Helen walked in, they were relieved to see Melchor sitting up on his hospital bed with a smile on his face. A flower arrangement sat on the bedside table, adding color and liveliness to the stark-white hospital room, next to mandarin oranges and *ensaymada*—a soft, buttered brioche sprinkled with sugar and shredded cheese.

"Danny, I'm glad you made it okay. I was so worried," Melchor said.

"When are you leaving this place?" Helen asked.

"The doctor is keeping me for at least another day for observation. But if you ask me, I'm ready to get out of here."

"How did you know that meeting with the guide was a trap?" Danny asked.

"I mistakenly gave you a number that was given to me by one of the military officials who interviewed me after I was taken off the *Desert Sea*. I was checking all my incoming messages when I woke up and noticed that the number wasn't the same as the one Commander Berto had given me," Melchor said. "I began to suspect the worst and so texted you right away."

"Great," Helen said. "Now, Dr. Klein knows our every move."

"Do you have any idea where Blake is?" Danny asked.

"The country has more than 7,100 islands and Blake could be hidden on any one of them. There are close to a hundred million people in the Philippines. I think it would be impossible to find him. It's time to let the government officials handle the rest. I really don't know what to do next."

"Can't you text the go-between?" Danny asked, frustration building in his voice.

"I'm afraid that even the go-between's phone number is compromised and that you two would end up dead the next time you run into Dr. Klein and his men. I think we're out of options and it would be best if we stand on the sidelines and watch the events play out. But first things first…we need to get rid of your phones. I'm pretty sure someone is monitoring you every time you make a phone call or send a text, tracking your every move."

Melchor opened the drawer in his bedside table and pulled out two new cellphones.

"I had one of my assistants get new phones. These are clean. I already preprogrammed my number on the phones so we can send text messages freely. Can I have your old ones?"

Danny and Helen gave Melchor their phones. With a pair of tiny screwdrivers, Melchor opened the backs of the phones and took the batteries out.

"There you go," Melchor said. "You two are officially off the grid."

"Thank you," Helen said.

"Is there anyone you can think of we can trust? Certainly, only a small percentage of the military is corrupt. Not all of them can be easily bribed?"

"I'll see what I can do. But now, the Cube," Melchor said, looking at the rollaway luggage by Danny's feet. "Someone might rob you at gunpoint thinking there's something valuable in it. Deposit it in a safety deposit box for safekeeping while we figure out our next move."

"Can you recommend a reputable place?" Helen asked.

"My driver will take you to a bank in Makati."

MAKATI WAS UNIQUE compared to the other

neighborhoods in Metro Manila. The streets were clean, lined with palm trees. Tall buildings rose on every block. Streets lights operated in synchronous timing, orchestrating the traffic flow. The drivers stopped at the red light and only proceeded when it turned green. Except for the occasional Jeepney, the city was practically a miniature America.

Two bank security guards armed with 12-gauge, pump-action shotguns opened the door when Danny and Helen walked up to the entrance.

A slightly overweight man in a white shirt and a red tie approached them.

"I am the bank's manager. I hear you are interested in renting a safety deposit box."

"I need the largest box available," Helen said.

"How big is the item you need to store?" the manager asked.

Danny pointed to the rollaway next to him. "We need to store the items inside for safekeeping. Less than a week."

After filling out the necessary forms and paying the required fees, the manager led them to the vault where rows of shiny deposit boxes were tightly sealed. Danny inspected the two empty boxes on the table.

"You may deposit your items in the boxes and then put the box in the appropriate slot. Call me when you're done so we can lock them together," the bank manager instructed.

After the bank manager left, Danny unzipped the rollaway luggage and carefully arranged the vacuum-sealed packages of Rx-18 compound into the two safety deposit boxes. Helen closed the flat, stainless steel doors and locked them.

"We're done!" Helen said.

"Might as well withdraw some cash. We will need money to get around."

"What's next?"

"I really don't know."

"Can you take me to a Catholic church while we're waiting for Melchor to call us?" Helen asked, reaching for Danny's hand. "I need to pray."

THEY ENTERED INTRAMUROS, which simply meant "within the walls." Its high walls measured approximately four medium-sized men standing on top of each other in height, about one and a half fathoms in thickness, and stretched three miles around. The bastion was built by the Spanish to ward off foreign invaders and to separate themselves from any unrest outside the city. With the Pasig River roping around its outskirts, the fortress was destroyed in World War II by the American forces while taking the city back from the Japanese Imperial Army.

Inside the walled city was San Agustin Church, the oldest stone church built by the Augustinian Friars in the early 1600s. Danny and Helen were walking up the church entrance when a girl in a dirty dress with innocent-looking eyes selling stringed *sampaguita* (jasmine flowers) came up to Helen.

Helen reached in her pocket and handed the girl a hundred-peso bill. The girl smiled and in exchange gave Helen two dozen *sampaguitas*.

"*Salamat po,*" the girl said with a wide smile on her face.

"She said 'thank you,'" Danny translated to Helen.

The church's interior was spacious. He marveled at the low-relief artwork on the high ceiling of ovals and squares and the massive chandeliers hanging above. The sight of Jesus with his outstretched hands and crown of thorns being nailed to the cross at the altar was humbling. The pulpit to his right hung like a capsule with its ornate design, where priests of the past had preached the day's teachings in Latin, which, more than likely, none of the worshippers understood.

Danny and Helen sat in one of the dark brown pews and faced the massive altar while thoughts of Blake's suffering in the hands of Commander Berto worried them. Helen knelt on the kneeling board, clasping her hands and bowing down. Danny silently sat next to her with eyes closed, thinking about the massive roadblock in front of them with no idea on how to proceed. He wished that he had never invented the Cube so that Blake would never have been kidnapped. Instead of making progress that would lead to Blake's rescue, their efforts to reach out to him had backfired, and their situation was worse than when they started more than a week ago.

Though Danny was baptized as a Catholic in his childhood, he rarely went to church. Yet now, here in this sacred place, he bowed his head and asked for forgiveness for not coming to church as often as he should. He prayed and asked the Almighty to help locate Blake and bring him back to safety and promised that in exchange for his friend's safe return, he'd dedicate his time and knowledge of the ocean to help stop the depletion of fisheries around the word.

THE DRIVER DROPPED THEM OFF at the Bay Palms Hotel's front entrance. They entered not knowing how many nights they would be spending in their room while they waited for the painstakingly slow process of hostage negotiation.

The hundred-year-old hotel glistened in the hot Manila afternoon with its dramatic white walls and royal blue roofs. Danny approached the front desk. The decorations of light varnished walls and polished brass handlebars seemed to be a remnant of the colonial era. For a brief moment, he felt transported back to the American and Japanese colonial days when Filipinos were treated like second-class citizens in their own country.

"We have a reservation under Melchor Rodriguez," Danny said.

"Sir, we have rooms available with two double beds or

with a king-size bed. Which one would you prefer?"

Danny turned to Helen.

"A king-size bed would be great," Helen replied.

Danny approached the window facing Manila Bay. He could make out the tadpole-shaped Corregidor Island in his mind—the military outpost that had guarded the entrance to Manila Bay against invaders.

He thought to himself it may be better if they returned to San Diego and let the Philippine authorities do their job and accept whatever the outcome may be. He could always make another batch of the Cube. Besides, he already knew that no one could replicate the Cube the way he envisioned it because the secret in making an effective batch lay in the process and not in the raw materials that go into it. It wouldn't matter if Commander Berto got his hands on it, NBH Fishing Industries would soon learn that reverse engineering his invention wasn't going to be easy. What was important now was to get to the U.S. Embassy and tell the officials about Dr. Klein's involvement with Blake's kidnapping so an arrest warrant could be issued. That way, Dr. Klein and his gang would back off from them.

Danny climbed on the bed next to Helen, lying on her back and staring directly up at the ceiling. She laid her head on his arm. It was the end of the line for both of them and there wasn't much that they could do but to follow the instructions from the government officials. With that notion, Danny felt that both of them had hit rock bottom. The only way to get Blake back alive was to get out of the way and let the people in charge handle the situation.

Just then his phone vibrated in his pocket. Danny sat up on the bed expecting that Melchor had already contacted the government officials and was ready to give them instructions on what to do next.

"Melchor," Danny answered, his heart beating in his chest.

"I just remembered meeting the general in the army who had organized an elite squad to hunt down the bomb makers in Mindanao several years ago. I believe he knows a lot about Commander Berto's activities," Melchor said.

"What do you want us to do?"

"I'd like you two to meet with him tonight. He's hosting a fundraising event in his old mansion in the city of Malolos. Each attendee is expected to make a donation and to dress up in a traditional Filipino costume to commemorate the past. Since we're pressed for time, you two need to attend his gala and find a way to talk to him privately and ask him to help you."

"But we don't have an invitation," Danny said.

"I've already arranged everything and the head of his charity is already expecting you but you must stop by the tailor for your Barong Tagalog and for Helen's traditional Filipina gown."

"When do you want us to go?"

"Go to the hotel concierge, rent a car and leave right away."

DANNY AND HELEN were greeted as soon as they walked into the tailor shop by the owner who had a mop top haircut that looked like a throwback from the sixties with a stud earring on his left ear.

"*Magandang hapon po*," the man said.

"Good afternoon to you, too," Danny responded. "Melchor sent us here. I need to be fitted for a Barong Tagalog and she needs a gown for the evening."

"Oh, yes. I've been expecting you. Come this way, please."

Danny stood straight on top of a raised platform surrounded by mirrors. With a measuring tape, the tailor measured the size of his neck and the length of his arms.

"You're unusually tall for a Filipino. Hopefully, I have your size," the tailor said, as he disappeared in the back.

When the tailor returned, he was holding a Barong Tagalog. The long-sleeved shirt was made of a transparent fabric and was decorated with an intricate embroidery pattern on the front of the shirt.

"I haven't worn one of these since I left the country," Danny said.

"You wear it over a white T-shirt and it goes well with black pants," the tailor said.

"How come it goes over the pants and not tucked in?" Danny asked.

"The Spanish colonizers back in the old days required the lower class to wear it untucked."

The tailor held up the Barong Tagalog while Danny

slipped it on. He stepped in front of the full-size mirror and studied himself. "The fabric is thin."

"It's a translucent fabric—usually made from pineapple leaves—which was designed to show that that no weapon is hidden under it."

When it was Helen's turn to get measured for her dress size, she stood up straight while the tailor wrapped the tape measure around her back and chest, stomach, hips and finally the length from her shoulder all the way down to her ankle.

"38-26-38. And your height's about five feet seven inches. Not much taller than most Filipino women. I think I have a ready-made dress that would fit you perfectly with only a few minor alterations."

A few minutes later, he emerged from the back room carrying several dresses by the hanger.

"This is called a *Terno*, a traditional yet slightly modern look of the Filipina gown. The other one is called a *Maria Clara* gown. It's more of a colonial-period dress named after the *mestiza* character from Dr. José Rizal's book *Noli Me Tangere*, which exposed the abuses of Spanish rule and the clergy. Would you like to try them on?"

"They're both beautiful," Helen said as she walked back to the dressing room.

When she came back, she was wearing the Maria Clara dress. It looked complicated with its various different pieces, consisting of a long skirt with yellow and black stripes, a blouse with medium-length sleeves and a translucent scarf that wrapped around her shoulder. Her hair was up. Danny stared at her with a new intensity as he marveled at her new look. She flicked the folding fan open with a smooth wrist action and playfully hid a part of her face.

"You look nice in that dress," Danny said.

"I'll try the other dress," she said, walking back to the dressing room.

Danny was already feeling comfortable in his Barong Tagalog when Helen emerged from the dressing room wearing the yellow Terno dress. The dress tapered down to her waist and then widened from her knees all the way down to her ankles. She turned to her side as she looked over the arc-shaped broad sleeves that slightly rose over her shoulders and caught her reflection in the mirror.

"This dress is so unique from the other dresses I've worn in the past."

"The sleeves are sometimes called butterfly sleeves," the tailor said.

"I think I would like to wear this one," Helen replied.

AT THE DOMESTIC section of the Manila airport, Dr. Klein compared the tail number on the twin engine parked on the tarmac to the picture on his phone that one of his men took back in Jolo airport. Confident it was the airplane he was looking for, he walked up to the two men fueling the aircraft.

"Excuse me. Do you know who owns this airplane? I'm

interested in hiring one for an upcoming trip," Dr. Klein casually asked.

One of the workers told him that it was owned by Magiting Aviation and pointed to the hangar located at the far end of the terminal. Dr. Klein politely thanked the man and hurried to the office.

The office was empty when Dr. Klein and his two assistants walked in the front door. He tapped the bell on the desk to call someone's attention. While waiting, he scanned the large map of the Philippines on the wall and felt a bit frustrated that he had been chasing Danny across the country but still hadn't caught him. The pilot who flew Danny and Helen to Jolo Island and back to Manila emerged from the back room. He was wearing a white button-down shirt, a three-bar epaulet on the shoulders and navy blue pants. One of Dr. Klein's assistants, the burly man with the curly hair, immediately recognized the pilot as the one who helped Melchor get on the plane and nodded to Dr. Klein. Wasting no more time, Dr. Klein lifted his shirt and showed the pilot the gun tucked in the front of his pants.

"I need you to tell me where I can find Professor Rodriguez," Dr. Klein asked with a straight face.

"Who are you?" the pilot asked.

"Let's say either someone who is about to do business with you or someone who is going to blow your brains out."

The pilot's eyes widened with fear.

"I really don't know where he is. He just showed up at the airport with a couple of people. No one tells me anything. My job is just to fly people to their destination. I don't ask any questions."

"Not a good answer," Dr. Klein said, reaching for his gun.

"Isn't he in the hospital? Why don't you look for him there?"

"There's a gazillion hospitals in Metro Manila. I don't have time to comb through every one of them."

Scared for his own safety and running out of options, the pilot fished his phone out of his pocket and scrolled through it until finding the driver's number who picked up Danny and Helen when they arrived earlier in the afternoon.

"I'm really sorry but this is all I have. You can ask the driver where the Professor is."

Dr. Klein, sensing that the pilot was telling the truth, put his shirt back over his gun. "If you're fucking with me, I'll come back here and kill you. Got it?"

Ten

THEY EVENTUALLY ARRIVED in Malolos—a city in the province of Bulacan—though it took them almost another hour to get out of Manila's congested traffic. After parking the fire-red SUV on the side of the mansion, Danny stepped out of the vehicle, reached for Helen's hand, and assisted her down. She looked elegant in her yellow Terno gown.

The mansion was large and had a rather grandiose aura to it. The bottom floor was made of bricks and concrete, while the second story was constructed of wood with large sliding windows made of a square-pattern of semitransparent capiz shells. The windows were opened all the way, allowing maximum cross ventilation to quell the hot and humid tropical summer.

Some of the guests were arriving in a *kalesa*—a horse-drawn carriage with large wheels with yellow spokes. The women entering the mansion wore Maria Clara gowns with silk umbrellas resting on their shoulders, looking elegant as the men looked noble in their transparent Barong Tagalog shirts.

"Glad I picked a nice gown," Helen said.

The host was waiting by the main entrance wearing loose red trousers and a long-sleeved shirt rolled up to his elbows. He escorted Danny and Helen straight to the back of the mansion. The courtyard was surrounded with rows of orange gumamela flowers, ferns and bamboo. Guests chattered among themselves with drinks in their hands. Since they knew no one at the party, Danny and Helen stood around idly listening to the *rondalla*—a string orchestra comprised of guitar, banduria and octavina players playing a traditional Tagalog song. A server with a tray of cantaloupe drinks and avocado shakes approached the couple.

"This party is impressive," Helen commented as she took as sip of the avocado shake.

"It reminds me of celebrating *Nochebuena* when I was young," Danny replied.

"What's that?"

"Christmas Eve. We would eat *queso de bola*, which is an Edam cheese ball, ham, and steamed rice cake wrapped in banana leaves. We would also hang a *parol*—a kind of star-shaped lantern—outside the house."

They were halfway through their drinks when elderly gentleman wearing a Barong Tagalog walked up to them with a slight limp. Thinking he was the man that they needed to meet, Danny said, "Good afternoon, General Rosales."

"Oh no. Not me. I'm the one in charge of the fundraising. Call me Martin."

"Is it possible to see him now? It's regarding an urgent matter," Helen said, handing him an envelope containing five hundred dollars in cash as their donation to the Preservation Society of Historic Homes and Churches.

"Let's go see him now," Martin said.

When Danny and Helen arrived, General Rosales was standing in the middle of the living room next to a large table made of Philippine mahogany. He was slightly shorter than Danny but had a large frame that told of an army man who had spent his entire military career on the field. Yet from his thick eyeglasses, Danny could tell that he was a scholar as well.

"General, these are the people your friend, Professor Rodriguez, spoke to you about," Martin said.

"It's nice to meet you," General Rosales said, offering his hand.

"Thank you for taking the time out of your busy day to talk to us," Danny said, gingerly reaching for his hand. "My name is Danny and I'm an oceanographer from California."

"And who would you be?" Mr. Rosales asked, turning to Helen.

"Helen Glass."

As much as Danny wanted to get straight to the point, he knew it was better to ease into the conversation. Even though Americans don't typically beat around the bush when conducting business, this attitude was frowned upon in most Asian countries. In fact, most of the time it was construed as downright rude, so Danny circumnavigated the real reason for their visit with the general.

"General," Danny said.

"Please, just call me Manoy. It's easier to pronounce than my real name. I've retired from the army already. I'm just an ordinary citizen now."

"Is that your nickname?" Helen asked.

"Yes. Short for Manuel. It makes me feel younger. We Filipinos like to use nicknames a lot," General Rosales said, reaching for a glass of water from the table.

"I'm honored to be here and impressed by what you are doing here to keep our traditions alive. Events like this will help ensure that future generations won't forget about our past. Helen was impressed by your reenactment of this important period of Philippine history," Danny said.

"It is my pleasure to have you as my guests. You look elegant in your Terno. But, if I may ask, why aren't you wearing a Maria Clara?" General Rosales said, looking straight at Helen.

"I almost picked one out while we were at the tailoring shop, but I just fell in love with this gown's wide sleeves."

"Maria Clara was actually one of the characters in a famous book. She is the symbol of Filipina femininity. But she was supposedly half-white."

"The tailor mentioned this to us in the store," Danny said.

"Wearing the Maria Clara instead of the Terno would have been more appropriate for you since you are white," General Rosales said.

"Maybe I will have the chance to wear one at your next party."

The general smiled at her remark.

"You have a very accomplished family, sir," Danny commented, looking up at the many laminated diplomas hanging on the wall.

"My children's little attainments," General Rosales said, trying to be humble.

"It's not easy to graduate from a four-year university," Helen added.

"Education is a gift we can give our children that can never be taken away. My son is now a lawyer with a practice in Manila, and my daughter graduated with an accounting degree and now lives in Canada with her husband and children. My wife and I fly to Toronto whenever we miss our grandchildren."

"Do you ever think of living abroad?"

"Oh, that's not for me. We may have many problems in this country, but this is where I belong."

General Rosales' phone rang.

"Excuse me," he said as he walked into the adjacent room.

When he was out of earshot, Helen turned to Danny.

"Can't you just get to the point and tell him why we're here?"

"You can't just tell people what's on your mind right off the bat. It's not how things are done here."

"We don't have time. The longer this takes, the longer Blake suffers."

"The general knows we didn't come here just to hear the rondalla play. The last thing we need is to look like ugly Americans walking into his house demanding favors and accommodations. You have to understand...he has nothing at stake here. He doesn't care what happens to Blake and has no motivation to help us. Please trust me. Just smile and follow my lead. Beating around the bush is a sport everyone here is expected to play. And to get Blake back we need to play it well," Danny said.

They heard the general's footsteps growing louder.

Danny and Helen went back to playing their parts, admiring the large portrait of a military man posing with his blue uniform and sword.

"That's Emilio Aguinaldo, a fearless young general renowned for his battles against the Spaniards," General Rosales said, entering the room. "He started fighting as just a young man without much knowledge in military tactics. But with great bravery and leadership he persevered and won many battles against the occupiers."

"You eventually won your freedom from Spain, right?" Helen asked.

"With the help of the United States, the first Philippine Republic was established in 1898. Actually, just a few miles away from here at the Barasoain Church our founders wrote the first Malolos Constitution. It is said that everyone on that day dressed in his or her best costume to celebrate our independence. Just like what you see here today. It was an important time in our history that I'm trying to keep alive by perpetuating our customs and traditions. Unfortunately, the new Philippine government roughly lasted for two years."

"That's when the new republic started fighting the Americans, isn't it?" Danny asked. Though he was well versed in the country's history, he wanted to keep the general talking.

"Yes…the Philippine-American War lasted about three years, and the United States ultimately became our new colonizer. We endured more than forty years of American rule. The Americans did send teachers and opened up education for everyone, but we wanted to rule ourselves. And just when we were on the right track to independence, the Japanese invaded in 1941. And then Imperial Japan became our newest occupiers. It wasn't until the end of World War II that the Philippines finally became independent."

General Rosales' cell phone rang again. He fished it out of his pocket and answered the call.

"I think I'm needed outside. My guests will be insulted if I don't spend more time shaking hands, kissing cheeks and making toasts."

With General Rosales leaving the room, Danny knew he had to make his move. There was no more time to waste.

"General, I almost forgot to mention but Professor Rodriguez spoke so highly of your proud service to our country. Perhaps, by now, you've realized we didn't really come here just for the roast pig?"

"How may I be of assistance?"

"My best friend, who happens to be her cousin, was kidnapped by Kulog ng Timog while conducting research in the Sulu Sea. I believe you had several encounters with their ruthless leader in the past while you were in Mindanao. We were hoping that you might help us get in touch with Commander Berto. We know it is a lot to ask, but the situation has become desperate."

"Oh, I like to help when I can but I'm retired now. It's been five years since I've worn battle fatigues. I'm afraid that I've been out of the loop on Kulog ng Timog's latest tactics and techniques. All I can say for sure is that Commander Berto has been in the kidnapping business for as long as I can remember. Although he's a greedy bastard, he doesn't just do it for the money. He's working to expand his influence in the region. I am sorry but I can't help you. If I were you, I'd let the Philippine government handle it. I'm sure that they're already aware of the situation and negotiating for his release. In fact, there is a small American detachment in Mindanao. They can help too."

"They are aware of the situation but we're afraid that my friend might get killed if the demands are not met."

"If it's money he's asking for, let the negotiators do their job. They deal with this kind of crisis all the time."

"Commander Berto is not only asking for money, but also a compound that I had developed as an oceanographer."

General Rosales put his fingers under his chin. His eyebrows joined in the middle.

"Now that you mention it, I do know a military officer who was involved in the release of a Korean hostage a year ago. He might be able to help you. If not, he'll at least steer you to the right people. He's currently in Baguio City teaching at the Philippine Military Academy. If you would like to meet with him, I'd gladly give him a call and tell him I sent you."

"Thank you, that would be extremely helpful, General," Helen said, glad to hear the news.

"His name is Captain Santos. He's my compadre. I'm one of his daughter's godparents. When are you planning to go to Baguio?"

"Tomorrow would be great. We're running out of time and need to resolve this crisis fast," Danny replied.

"Great. Then sleep here tonight. The traffic driving back to Manila will be a nightmare. You'll waste more than three hours in traffic. This is a ten-bedroom mansion and we are accustomed to having guests stay with us.

Earlier we had a cancelation, and since you have already been so generous with your donation, it would be our pleasure to have you stay here. Enough talk…now it's time to eat the *lechon*! Be sure to try the skin. It's crispy like *chicharon* but tastes a hundred times better."

They walked downstairs.

DR. KLEIN ARRIVED with his two assistants in tow in the Chinatown section known as Binondo, trying with hurried footsteps to dodge the oncoming masses of people meandering in every direction. The narrow streets were lined with restaurants displaying steam buns in bamboo steamers and roast ducks hanging on hooks. Herb shops sold cure-alls for various ailments and a small furniture shop displayed a large vase and a wooden table set.

When Dr. Klein and his men walked in the front door of the restaurant, he spotted the driver they had been searching for eating a plate of pansit noodles. With no time for formalities, Dr. Klein sat down in front of the driver and stared him straight in the face.

"Do I know you?" the driver asked, putting his fork down.

"Maybe we can do business together."

"Regarding?"

"Information," Dr. Klein said, lighting up a cigarette.

"I'm just a driver for hire."

"That's exactly why I'm here. Can you tell me where to find that couple you picked up from the airport?"

"The American woman and the tall Filipino guy?"

"Exactly. Where did you drop them off?"

The driver shifted his head and looked around his surroundings, feeling a sudden uneasiness in Dr. Klein's presence.

"I'm paid to drive people to their destinations and leave."

"Maybe this will help you remember where you took them," Dr. Klein said as he pushed a stack of thousand-peso bills across the table. "You only have to tell us where you took them and you will never see me again."

"You come here to insult me?"

"Here's more for your troubles," Dr. Klein said, adding several more bills to the table. "I strongly suggest you take the money, or my friends might just take you for a trip to Pasig River. Who knows where your body might be found in the morning."

The driver glanced up at the two men standing over the table eyeing him with violent intent. Though his eyes trembled with fear, after a few seconds of silence, the driver pocketed the cash.

"They are staying at the Bay Palms Hotel. I dropped them off around two."

"And how do I make sure you're telling the truth? Just so I'd go away?"

"Professor Rodriguez called me a few hours ago but I missed it...listen," the driver said, pressing play on his phone's voicemail.

"Can you pick up Danny and Helen at the Bay Palms Hotel? They are on the fifth floor in a room facing the ocean."

"But they're not there right now."

"Do you know where they're at?" Dr. Klein asked, his face contorting into a look of impatience.

"When I called back, Professor Rodriguez told me that I was too late and they had already driven themselves to a mansion in Malolos for some sort of festival. Maybe they'll be back tonight…I don't know?"

DR. KLEIN and his two assistants walked straight to the pool area at the Bay Palms Hotel, pretending to be one of the many guests cooling off in the balmy night. When two women in their bathing suits walked out of the hotel's rear entrance, Dr. Klein rushed to the door, acting as if he had forgotten his keycard and casually walked in. A few minutes later, when no one was looking, he let his assistants in.

Dr. Klein checked the room number and pressed his ear to the door, listening for any activity but heard no noise from inside. Anticipating that Danny and Helen might be in bed sleeping, he signaled his men to draw their guns just in case the two decided to push their way out of the room. He inserted a fake key card attached to a handheld electronic device. Pressing several buttons on the keypad, a few seconds later the door clicked open.

Disappointed to discover that the room was empty,

they fanned out in the room and searched for the rollaway containing the Cube. Dr. Klein pulled the dresser drawers open while his two assistants searched through the bathroom. There was no sign of the Cube. Disappointed that he didn't find what he came for, Dr. Klein sat on the high, winged-back chair next to the window, rested his gun on his lap, and watched the ships and freighters with their bright lights squeeze through Manila Bay. Then, he waited for Danny and Helen to walk through the front door.

Eleven

THE FOLLOWING DAY, they left the city of Malolos. Danny was behind the wheel of the SUV feeling jittery as he drove, trying not to get hit by the tricycles coming at them from every direction. Though the sun was still rising, the streets were already teeming with activities. The small, family sari-sari stores were ready and open for business. As the SUV bounced up and down the pothole-laden streets, Helen anxiously programmed their destination onto her portable GPS screen.

They soon made it to the North Luzon Expressway that would take them straight to Baguio City where the Philippine Military Academy was located. The Metro Manila four-lane highway was already clogged with container trucks, trucks carrying sugarcane, buses overflowing with passengers, and private vehicles leaving for work downtown.

Danny stole a glance at Helen. She was quiet but constantly shifting her weight in her seat and staring out the window at the row upon row of three-story billboard signs. They saw mile after mile of larger-than-life signs with clear-skinned models advertising the latest skin care products, sexy-fitting jeans and whitening toothpastes. Then there were pictures of happy families encouraging people to call an agent for one of the hippest, newest and tallest condominium complexes. Finally, came the posters showing a handsome, black-haired, copper-skinned leading man who was Filipino cinema's latest discovery, just about to seductively kiss his leading lady in an effort to promote their latest romantic comedy.

As they got farther away from the major towns, the sky began to open up, revealing blazing white clouds scattered across the light topaz sky. There were now rice fields flooded in water for irrigation that reflected the sun in between columns of freshly planted rice stalks. In the far distance, a carabao, or water buffalo, pulled a plow while a barefoot farmer trailed behind, mindless of the cars speeding by.

CARVED INTO THE side of a mountain, the road up to Baguio City was steep as it constantly wound back and forth. The SUV was approaching a switchback when the traffic began to slow down. Cars and vans began stopping on the side of the road. Tourists were taking pictures in front of a large statue of a lion's head.

Just as the SUV started moving again, Danny glanced at his side-view mirror, noticing a yellow sedan about six cars behind trying to pass a truck carrying sacks of sugar. If it hadn't been for the reckless way that the yellow sedan was trying to pass the cars in front of it, Danny wouldn't have suspected anything out of the ordinary. But the car's urgent, erratic movements were alarming, considering most drivers on two-lane Kennon Road were aware of the mountain's dangerous turns. His gut told him that something just wasn't right.

"I think we've got company."

Helen looked behind her. The expression on her face quickly changed from worry to panic. "I just saw Dr. Klein in a yellow car."

"How close are they?" Danny asked.

"The car has just passed a large bus," Helen said. "They're five cars back."

Not wanting another encounter with Dr. Klein and his gunmen, Danny stepped on the gas. The SUV zoomed forward and started to gain distance from the cars behind. Seeing that the oncoming traffic was clear, he quickly passed the truck in front of him. For the next several miles, Danny maneuvered around cars but the yellow sedan seemed to mirror his actions. Each time he gained distance, the yellow sedan managed to close the gap. He knew that Dr. Klein wouldn't stop until he caught up to them.

After passing a flatbed truck, Danny steered the SUV

up the ascending road. He could see a deep gorge to his right and knew that they could easily fall if he made a mistake and overcorrected the steering wheel.

Soon the yellow sedan fell further back until Danny could no longer see it from his rearview mirror. As they climbed to almost 5,000 feet, the surroundings became noticeably greener with the trees that covered the mountainside—the temperature dropping to the high 60s.

Danny glanced in his rearview mirror and, to his shock, saw Klein's yellow sedan moving faster up the mountain. The distance between them was decreasing with each passing second.

"See anything?" Danny asked. Sweat formed on his temples.

"They're right behind us!" Helen shouted.

Through the side-view mirror, Danny saw an arm sticking out of the sedan's front passenger seat and a pistol's muzzle pointed directly at them. He floored it. The SUV belched smoke as it struggled to climb up the mountain. Gunshots echoed across the Cordillera mountain range. There was nowhere to go but forward and fast. The only way to evade Dr. Klein's wrath was to outrace him.

As they reached Baguio City, the road forked and Danny saw his one and only opportunity to lose Dr. Klein. To the right was the road leading directly to the Philippine Military Academy entrance gate. But it was a one-way road and offered no place to hide if Dr. Klein caught up to them. Even if Danny could outrun his pursuer, Dr. Klein would quickly figure out they were headed to the Military Academy—and with only one road leading in and out— Dr. Klein was sure to be waiting for the couple on their way back. Danny decided to risk it all and stay on Kennon Road. It was a straight shot to the city and he hoped that once they arrived that there would be plenty of places to hide and lose him for good.

Their SUV was still in the lead but Klein's yellow sedan was only two cars back and quickly gaining ground.

The SUV's passenger side-view mirror suddenly exploded.

"Get down!" Danny shouted.

Danny steered erratically as he weaved in and out of the lanes, trying to prevent their tires from being punctured by the barrage of bullets coming at them from behind. They came up behind a truck carrying a massive load of sand. Danny felt trapped and knew that whatever he did, Dr. Klein would follow and still catch up. Danny stepped on the gas and pulled in front of the sand truck to shield the SUV's tires. Through his rearview mirror, Danny saw the yellow sedan's front bumper trying to jump into the opposite lane to pass the truck but the oncoming traffic was nonstop. Dr. Klein couldn't find a break in the parade of cars leaving the city.

As they grew closer to Baguio City, Danny noticed the gaps between the cars were widening. It was only a matter of time before the yellow sedan would be in shooting range again. This long stretch of road was a deathtrap because they would soon be out in the open with no place to hide. Danny had to act quickly or they were sure to be captured. Not knowing where to go, he steered the SUV in the direction of Burnham Park. His only hope was the presence of kids riding their bikes and lovers rowing boats like swans on the lake would dissuade Dr. Klein from gunning them down. Danny tried to blend in with traffic but the merging vehicles getting in between them were both a blessing and a curse.

"The yellow sedan is still following us," Helen said.

He looked behind him. At least ten cars were sandwiched between them.

Danny prayed that the quagmire of cars, trucks and Jeepneys in front of him would start moving so they could get away. They were in a dire situation with no real options left, and so Danny took a chance and turned down a narrow street hoping it would somehow lead them to safety.

Out of the corner of his eye, Danny saw an alleyway between two commercial buildings and turned onto a one-way street. To his dismay, a man pushing a cart full of handicrafts crossed their path. Acutely aware that in their rapidly deteriorating situation stopping would be suicide, he honked his horn and pressed harder on the gas pedal instead of slamming on the brakes. The man pushing the cart was startled and desperately tried to stop his forward momentum, pulling back his cart to avoid being hit.

Danny was able to squeeze the SUV through the narrow space between the edge of the curb and the cart's front end. The cart's front crashed into the SUV's rear bumper. Handicrafts consisting of wicker baskets, bamboo chimes, mats made from hemp ropes, brooms made from soft reeds, chandeliers made of sea shells, and a man's wood carving in a barrel were strewn all over the alleyway.

"They'll eventually catch up to us and soon," Danny said.

"We need to get off the street, ditch the car and flee from this place!" Helen screamed.

Danny surveyed his surroundings and quickly formed an escape plan.

"Hang on!" he shouted.

Danny switched the gearstick to second. The SUV lurched forward, one half of the vehicle on the street with the other on the sidewalk. He honked his horn warning the pedestrians to move out of the way. The vendors selling trinkets quickly grabbed what they could in order to save their wares from being crushed by the SUV's massive tires.

"Use the goddamn street, you idiot!" a merchant shouted.

Danny squeezed the SUV though a driveway in between two buildings and parked the SUV at the back of a hotel.

"What are you trying to do?" Helen asked.

"Get out now! We need to get as far away from Dr.

Klein as possible," Danny said, opening the door. Helen grabbed her backpack from the rear passenger seat and bolted out.

With their SUV concealed among the dozen or so parked guest vehicles, they ran straight into the hotel lobby and booked a night's room so that they could keep their vehicle on the premises.

DANNY AND HELEN NEEDED to get to Captain Santos right away. It was already 10 a.m. and they couldn't afford to dilly-dally. As they hurried toward the main street, they passed by the street vendors selling sweet fried bananas, dried squid, barbecued corn and hot dogs on a stick.

"Dr. Klein is still driving around looking for us. We can't be seen here," Helen said.

"We need to cut across this empty lot to get to the other street and get a taxi to take us to the Philippine Military Academy compound."

"THESE TWO AREN'T Harry Houdini. They couldn't have pulled a disappearing act on us that quick. They're just around here hiding. Keep looking!" Dr. Klein shouted at his men in frustration.

Dr. Klein and his men scanned the roads. With Danny's tall stature, he should have towered over most of the pedestrians on the sidewalk. And with Helen's light skin, he expected to be able to spot both of them right away.

"Go through there," Dr. Klein ordered the driver to go through the skinny two-way alley.

WHILE RUNNING ACROSS the empty lot, they encountered a dog frothing at the mouth, white with patches of brown all over its body. It started running in their direction at full speed. Danny scanned his immediate surroundings for a weapon. He saw an old rake lying on the dirt and picked it up.

"Danny!" Helen shouted.

"Get behind me!"

As the dog was about to lunge at them, Danny pointed the head of the rake with upturned teeth and tried to push the dog back.

THOUGH DR. KLEIN'S attention was focused on the people meandering the streets, hoping that either Danny or Helen would suddenly appear, the nasty dog, howling and barking from the open field caught his attention. He shifted his gaze to where the noise was coming from. To his delight, he saw Helen standing behind Danny while he tried desperately to push the dog back.

"Looks like Christmas came early," Dr. Klein said as a calculating smile formed on his mouth.

"STOP, YOU CRAZY ASS DOG!" Danny yelled.

Danny focused on the dog's eyes as it positioned itself

for attack. As if the dog was high on drugs, it opened its terrifying mouth with its sharp teeth glistening in the morning sun. Everything around him moved in slow motion. The last thing he wanted was to hurt the poor creature, but he didn't have any choice. Just in the nick of time, Helen pulled out an energy bar and threw it at the dog. The food instantly grabbed the dog's attention, and it stopped from barking and began chewing the energy bar.

Though Helen's quick thinking had preoccupied the dog, their relief was short lived when a familiar yellow sedan pulled up on the street.

"We need to get out of here fast," Danny said, dropping the rake. He directed her to run as far away as possible from the open field in order to blend in with the pedestrians on the sidewalks going about their day.

THERE WERE HUNDREDS of white taxis zooming along Session Road, but each one was full of passengers. Danny knew an empty taxi would eventually pass by, but it would be suicide to stand on the side of the road trying to flag one down with Dr. Klein and his men right behind them. Danny thought of hiding in one of the building's alleyways to wait until a taxi pulled up and dropped off a passenger, but that could chip away precious minutes.

A group of school children, led by their teacher, suddenly crossed the street. Traffic came to a halt. Just then, Helen saw an empty taxi directly in front of them.

"Let's go," she said, tugging on Danny's shirt.

They got in the backseat and quickly closed the door.

"Where do you want to go?" the driver asked.

"To the Military Academy compound," Danny said.

As soon as the driver set the meter on and the taxi started moving, a disco song about staying alive started blasting out the speakers. All that Danny could hope for was that they would still be alive when they got to their destination. He reached for Helen's hand. Both of them finally breathed a sigh of relief.

Twelve

THE ENTRANCE to the Philippine Military Academy looked like a castle's ramparts. Danny pulled Helen closer to him to make it look like they were a couple of tourists on a leisurely tour. The guard peered inside the taxi for a quick inspection and waved them through.

Not knowing where to find Captain Santos, Danny and Helen walked into what they thought was the administration building. Cadets in uniforms, consisting of black shoes, white pants, grey long-sleeve tops and red hats filled the building.

Danny walked up to a middle-aged woman with oval-shaped glasses sitting behind the desk.

"Ma'am, we're looking for Captain Santos."

"May I ask why?" the woman replied.

"It's a private matter," Helen said.

The woman's eyebrows rose as she fished for more

information.

"We're sent by General Rosales. I believe he has taught some courses here some years back when he was in active duty," Danny said.

"And how did you know him?" the woman asked.

"We attended his annual charity event last night. We need to deliver an important message to him," Helen added.

"Captain Santos is reviewing the cadets."

THE GRANDSTAND WAS FILLED with military personnel in their class-B uniforms when Danny and Helen arrived. The PMA silent drill team was performing in the open field. They sat in the upper seats and waited until the short program was over.

The cadets marched with rifles resting on their shoulders, their arms swinging in perfect unison, then stopped just in front of the grandstand, knees still rising and falling as they marched in place. Their chins jutted forward, chests out and shoulders pulled back like toy soldiers on a Christmas music box. The cadets formed a circle. In one fluid move, each cadet passed his rifle to the man to his right, creating a trick that the circle was rotating. The crowd cheered. For their next act, they spun their rifles and threw them behind. The cadet behind stepped forward and with perfect timing caught the falling rifle. The move was repeated several times. Their proficiency created the illusion of an undulating sea.

As soon as the presentation was over, the crowd stood up and headed for the exit. Danny and Helen proceeded directly to the middle of the grandstand where several high-ranking officials in their army-green and navy-white uniforms were gathered. Since neither Danny nor Helen knew what Captain Santos looked like, they asked a military man with lots of ribbons displayed on his left chest and wearing an ornately designed hat, who was standing in the mix of the officers.

"Good afternoon, sir. We're looking for Captain Santos," Danny asked, bowing his head to show humility.

The military man had a protruding stomach that suggested many years of good life.

"I'm Captain Santos."

"Sir. If you can please spare a minute, we have a few questions we'd like to ask you," Danny said.

"Is there something I can help you with?"

"We're here on behalf of General Rosales," Helen said.

The cordial expression on Captain Santos' face changed into a contorted look of confusion.

"I believe you might have mistaken me for someone else. I don't know anyone by that name."

General Rosales was in charge of the military operations in Mindanao a few years back. He told me that you served together," Danny said.

Danny felt his heart drop and a sickening feeling bubbling in his stomach. Maybe General Rosales had just told them a lie to brush them off and make them leave. It was a common trait for Filipinos not to say no directly to a person asking favors in order to save face from embarrassment. Usually one would instead get an answer like "I'll see what I can do" or "It might be difficult to do what you're asking". But General Rosales seemed to be sincere when he told them that he would help get them in touch with an official who had dealt with Commander Berto. Now Danny felt like he was making a fool of himself.

Captain Santos grew irritated. Helen sensed his annoyance and quickly tugged Danny's hand.

"Pardon us," Helen said.

"We're sorry for bothering you on your busy day. It must have been a big mix up," Danny said.

Just when Danny and Helen were about to leave, one of the officers interrupted. "There's another officer here named Captain Sando."

In an instant, Danny realized that General Rosales might have mispronounced Captain Santos for Captain Sando when he was rushing down to the courtyard.

"Perhaps he's the one we're looking for. Is he a doctor?" Helen asked.

"Yes. He leads a college volunteer group and just left for the Banaue Rice Terraces early this morning."

AN HOUR LATER, they retrieved the SUV from the small parking space where they had left it. Helen watched the city slowly disappearing in the side-view mirror as they drove away from the city of pines. She thought of their ordeal earlier with the crazy car chase up Kennon Road, the vicious dog that nearly ravaged them, and Dr. Klein's relentlessness to get his hands on the Cube. She wondered if Captain Sando would be able to give them any guidance to help them get in touch with Commander Berto. They were now going farther away from where Blake was being held captive and heading right into the Cordillera Mountain.

After driving more than five hours, they arrived at the Banaue Rice Terraces. *Ifugaos* were performing a traditional dance in the open field for backpackers. The male dancers wore red loincloths and brimless feathered hats. The women wore red and black striped skirts with white blouses. In a circle, they danced to the beat of brass cymbals clanging together in a rhythmic pattern. Slightly hunched over, their arms were outstretched like Philippine eagles soaring over the mountains.

Danny maneuvered the SUV down a narrow, two-lane road alongside a shallow creek running down from the mountain until reaching the place where Captain Sando and his group of students were supposed to be staying—the Sky Inn.

Danny approached the front desk clerk, a middle-aged man reading a newspaper and drinking coffee.

"*Kuya*, please forgive our rudeness. We're looking for Captain Sando. Is he here?" Danny asked.

"You also volunteers?"

"Kinda," Helen said.

"He is with his students where the Ifugaos live," the man said.

"Do you know where?" Helen asked.

The man motioned them to the balcony. The view from their vantage point was spectacular. From a distance, Banaue Rice Terraces looked like giant steps ascending into the sky. The rows of green rice stalks sprang out from the water. Though Danny had seen pictures in textbooks when he was in grade school, nothing prepared him for the grandeur of the 2,000-year-old masterpiece by the Ifugao tribe, who layered the mountains using rudimentary tools like wooden picks and shovels that were only available during their time.

"The rice terraces look amazing," Helen said.

"Beautiful, huh?" the man said. "It's the eighth wonder of the world. I know there's only seven but I think there should be eight. Do you see where that smoke is coming from?" the man said, pointing. "Captain Sando is there right now with his students."

Danny narrowed his eyes and focused on the small village framed by clumps of banana trees. There were no more than thirty houses perched on the side of the mountain. Most of houses were built from cinder blocks and corrugated roofs, while some were made in the traditional Ifugao design with tall, sloping thatched roofs.

"How do we get there?" Helen asked.

"Just go that way and it will lead you there," the man

answered, pointing to a trail going down the mountain.

Danny and Helen followed the path of stone steps descending towards the small village. They walked along a stream rolling down the mountain. A series of interconnected bamboo pipes diverted water to the terrace and flooded the flat plain. The residual water flowed down to the lower layer of another rice terrace below. Danny and Helen carefully walked along the stone wall that served as a dike to hold the water in and prevent the soil from eroding. The flowers along the way danced in the wind and green blades of rice leaves stood proudly under the dome of the bright sky.

CAPTAIN SANDO was sitting on the bench next to a board with various packages of medicine tacked to it. He was a thin man with clear brown skin and a sympathetic face. Danny and Helen quietly stood behind the villagers and the volunteer medical students gathered around him and listened without interrupting the presentation.

"This pink one is for your stomach. When you have headaches, you take this white pill. If you are ever confused, we have clinics you can go to that are staffed by nursing students and doctors," Captain Sando said, pointing to the medicines with a long stick.

From the expressions on the villagers' faces, they seemed confused with the variety modern medicines he was presenting.

The village elders stood up defiantly. "Why do we need

your medicines? For years, the medicine man has been treating our ailments through traditional methods with herbs and special plants."

Captain Sando countered. "You shouldn't stop using the medicinal plants that have been working for you, but because foreigners visit your villages, they can unfortunately bring diseases not native to you. New diseases need modern medicines to cure them."

When the presentation was over, the volunteer students broke up into small groups to teach the villagers how to get to the medical clinics set up in town.

Danny and Helen approached Captain Sando.

"Good afternoon, Captain," Danny said.

"Are you here to volunteer your services?" Captain Sando replied, puzzled.

"No, sir, we came here on behalf of General Rosales. I believe you two are good friends. We met him at the party he hosted yesterday."

"So you met my compadre, Manoy?"

"He told us to meet with you, sir," Helen added.

"What exactly are you here for?"

"Didn't he call you already?"

"Let me see," Captain Sando glanced at his phone and began reading the message out loud. *"Pards, see if you can help Danny and Helen. They came to see me asking for help yesterday but I couldn't. I hope you can do something for them."*

"We came to see General Rosales hoping he could help

up us get in contact with Commander Berto," Danny said.

"The leader of Kulog ng Timog? Why do you want to see him?" Captain Sando asked.

"His group kidnapped my best friend while he was conducting research in the Sulu Sea. We were hoping that General Rosales could help us but he said that he had already retired from the army and suggested to see you instead because you've dealt with this group in the past. Can you help us get in touch with him?"

"Aren't the Philippine authorities already handling this? I'm sure the last thing that the government wants is for another hostage to die."

"I think the U.S. and Philippine governments are already doing that but I'm afraid that my cousin might be killed during his rescue," Helen said. "We'd rather give into Kulog ng Timog's demands to get him back without further delay."

"How much is Commander Berto asking?" Captain Sando asked.

"A million dollars and a formula that I had developed," Danny said.

"I think you might have a bit of a problem. Commander Berto is not your typical outlaw operating in the southern Philippines. He almost always transports his hostages to a different location right away to avoid detection. This is what happened to the Frenchman they kidnapped sailing in the area two years ago. He was taken to one of the hundreds of tiny islands in the area. Most likely, your friend is now on the island of Basilan. If that's the case, then it would be very difficult for you two to reach him. Kulog ng Timog's camp is entrenched deep in the jungles and constantly moving. Even the army has difficulties locating them, despite the armored personnel carriers and helicopters at their disposal. I don't think I'm the right person to help you on this issue. I'm a military doctor, not a hostage negotiator."

The bad news hit Danny hard. He felt as if shotgun pellets had just blasted through his chest. Distraught, he sat down on the wooden bench to compose himself.

"Looks like we have no other choice but to head back to Manila and go directly to the U.S. Embassy, and tell them that Commander Berto is demanding the Cube as the ransom and let them solve it," Helen said.

"There might be another way to reach Commander Berto," Captain Sando added.

Danny looked up.

"How's that possible?"

"I was the doctor who treated the kidnapped Korean man after he was freed by Kulog ng Timog. I remember a go-between was involved in his release. He goes by the name 'Boy.'"

"Captain, it seems that every male in this country from age five to fifty is nicknamed 'Boy'. Do you have his exact name?"

"From what I remember, he owns a club in Olongapo City called Paradise East. His full nickname is 'Boy

Kulot'—Kulot means curly hair. Go see him and maybe he can help you."

"Thank you, Captain. This means a lot to us," Helen said, her eyes perking up.

"It's a long shot, but if he decides to help you he'll ask to get paid in return for his services," Captain Sando said.

"We came prepared, sir," Danny said.

"It's not going to be cheap."

BACK IN THE SUV, Danny dialed Melchor's number.

"Did you learn anything?" Melchor asked.

"We need to meet with the hostage negotiator. He lives in Olongapo City," Danny said.

"You're going when?"

"It would take us another six hours to get back to Baguio City and another four hours to Olongapo City. It will be dark soon and the roads are too dangerous to drive at night. Can you send the plane to pick us up and a driver to take the SUV back to Manila? I believe there's a local airport that's about two and a half hours away from here."

Thirteen

THE SPANIARDS first discovered Subic as a strategic military location, but it was the Americans who developed the thick-forested area southeast of the city of Olongapo into the biggest naval base outside the United States. The once-mighty fortress was where warships and nuclear-powered aircraft carriers were repaired for their seaworthiness. With the American lease on the land in limbo, combined with the destructive power of Mt. Pinatubo when it erupted, the place that the U.S. Navy called home for more than 60 years closed without much fanfare. At the end of 1992, the outpost that had become the symbol of American colonialism became history.

ROCK AND ROLL was seeping through the door at the front entrance of Paradise East when Danny and Helen arrived. The club was located in Magsaysay Drive—the main avenue slicing through the middle of Olongapo City and dividing the municipality into its eastern and western portions.

Danny pulled the large door handle. The putrid smell of cigarette smoke that clung to the walls and the stale stench of spilt beers on the linoleum floor greeted them. Danny coughed at the ghastly smell, and Helen covered her nose to prevent herself from gagging on the tobacco smell. The bouncer looked at them, raising his eyebrows.

"Twenty-five peso cover charge," the bouncer said.

"We're looking for Boy. Is he around?" Danny asked.

"You need to talk to him," the bouncer said, pointing with his lips to the man behind the bar.

Danny was about to step forward but the bouncer placed his hand on his chest.

"I said twenty-five pesos. Are you deaf?"

Danny fished a hundred-peso bill from his pocket and placed it in the bouncer's open hand.

On the way to the bar, Danny and Helen passed by the go-go dancers. Wearing long leather boots and bikini thongs, they swung their hips provocatively inside oversized birdcages with bored looks on their faces, entertaining tourists from Korea, Japan, Australia, and America. Danny looked to his right and noticed men of all ages sitting at the tables in the darkened part of the club, petite bar-girls with deep brown complexions and long, shiny hair sitting on their laps, chatting along with broken English.

"We're looking for Boy. I believe he owns the bar," Danny asked a muscular, light-skinned man wearing a short-sleeved, Hawaiian button-down.

"What's it to you?" the man asked gruffly.

Danny recognized a New York accent.

"Is he around?" Helen said.

"Let's say I'm his associate and any of his business is also my business. Now if you won't tell me why you're here then this conversation is over," the man said.

"Do you know Captain Sando?" Danny asked.

"Am I supposed to?" the man asked.

"Sir, let me apologize for our demeanor. We got off the wrong foot," Helen explained. "Perhaps you have heard the news about the American abducted in the southern Philippines?"

"I read the newspaper from time to time."

"We're here because we need his help locating Commander Berto. We just flew in from Banaue after meeting with Captain Sando. He told us that Boy was the negotiator who helped with the hostage's release two years ago."

The man's demeanor quickly changed from impatience to friendliness.

"You can call me Nick. I was part of the rescue effort. Is the American related to you?"

"Yes. He's my best friend and her cousin. He was in a research vessel operating on the Sulu Sea when the armed group of men took him," Danny said.

"Those damn kidnappers are giving this wonderful country a bad name. Every time something like this happens, tourists don't come. It affects many businesses, especially mine."

"We were hoping that Boy could help us locate Commander Berto and give him his ransom and get my cousin back," Helen intervened.

"Do you know that by paying what those thugs are demanding we're making things worse? They will only do this again," Nick said.

"I understand that. But what if your brother or your sister was kidnapped by those lawless men, and you had the money to pay for the ransom. Would you still think the same?" Helen said.

He placed his amber bottle of beer on the counter. "Boy is in the cockfighting arena right now. He's thin and short."

"Most Filipino men are thin and short. There must be at least a thousand people in there with that description. How will I recognize him?" Danny asked.

"He always sits by the ringside. He's a big fan of American football—you'll see him wearing a jersey. He's superstitious and thinks it gives him good luck."

THE NOISE IN THE ARENA was deafening when Danny and Helen walked in. They sat in the upper bleachers for a bird's eye view. Carefully, they inspected each person in the crowd, trying to isolate anyone with a jersey.

"I think he's that one down there by the ringside," Helen said. "Let's go see him now."

"No. Not now. Looks like he's passionate about cockfighting and I don't think he'll talk to us while he's still here. We'll just have to follow him out once the game is over."

The cockfighting aficionados, armed with cash in their pockets and a prayer from their patron saint, shouted in excitement as they rooted for their fighter. Since it was impossible to hear what the person on the other side of the arena was wagering, the bettors communicated through the pandemonium with hand gestures.

"What are these people shouting?" Helen asked, mystified.

"They're shouting '*wala o meron*'—'hat or no hat'. Do you see the two men down there? One has a hat on while the other one doesn't," Danny said, pointing to the fighting cocks' owners as they stroked the feathers of their prized possessions on a brown patch of soil in the middle of the arena. "They're betting."

The gamecocks were lowered to the ground. While the owners held their gamecock by the tail, they let the fighters peck at each other to excite their aggressions. Then the referee ordered the fight to commence. The owners released their fighters.

The feathers around their necks spread out like a lion's mane. The decibel level in the arena quadrupled. The hostile roosters pumped with vitamins and a concoction of energy-packed feeds lowered their heads to commence the fight for their lives. With wings spread and anger blazing in their faces, the roosters attacked each other with ferocity. Jumping high in the air, wings flapping, and with talons outstretched, they tried to rip each other's guts with fury. Equipped with three-inch blades, they swung their legs up and down and side to side hoping to cut their opponent's main artery and survive the fight to the death.

As the gamecocks jumped several feet up in the air from the packed soil, the gamblers nervously watched the roosters rhythmically perform the ancient death-dance of alpha male domination. The noise level in the arena exploded into another thunderous level.

A few minutes later, the dark brown rooster managed to maneuver on top of the white rooster and peck for the mortal blow. All that the rooster on the bottom could hope for was to be saved by the bell, but no such clang would ever come.

When the referee rushed in and separated them, the white-feathered rooster was covered in blood, motionless. The match was over. The referee hoisted the red-brown rooster up in the air. The winning side of the arena erupted with cheers knowing that there was money to be collected, while the lifeless body of the white rooster dripping with blood lay silently on the packed soil.

Boy got up from his seat and headed for the exit.

"Come on," Danny said to Helen.

"WHERE IS HE?" Helen asked, pushing her way through the waves of people leaving the arena.

Danny turned sideways, squeezing himself through the crowd to catch up with Boy. For a second, he lost Boy in the thick crowd. It was impossible to go any faster through the narrow exits and all he could do was wait for the line to move faster. He craned his neck hoping to see which direction Boy was heading toward, but with the new batch of people eager to get in the arena, it was difficult to spot him. Arms and elbows brushed up against his back and torso.

Concerned for Helen's safety and wanting to protect her from some of the perverts in the crowd who would seize the opportunity to touch her or press their bodies on her, he pulled her in front of him.

"If people start pushing, just press your palm against the person in front of you," Danny hurriedly said.

After making their way out of the arena, they frantically searched for Boy, hoping he was still in the periphery. By dumb luck, he saw Boy standing under the tree with a cigarette between his fingers.

"Pardon me for bothering you while you're having a smoke, but are you Boy Kulot?"

"Maybe?"

"My name is Danny. This is Helen. We just came from your club and were told we could find you here."

"Are you with the police?"

"No. We're here because Captain Sando told us about you." Helen said.

"I don't know anyone named Captain Sando. Why are you looking for me?" Boy said, throwing his cigarette butt on the ground and stepping on it.

"Captain Sando told us that you helped with the release of the hostage abducted by Kulog ng Timog."

"I don't do that anymore. All I want is to live in peace, running my club and going to cockfights."

"Mr. Boy," Helen said, "Commander Berto and his men kidnapped my cousin. We need your help with contacting him."

Boy said nothing and nonchalantly began to walk away from them.

"Please don't take this as rude, but we are willing to pay for any inconveniences and troubles if you help," Danny said.

"Think of it as a contribution to a good cause. We know that it takes money to get things moving," Helen added.

Boy stopped walking and turned to them. The annoyance and distrust carved into his face melted into a smile.

"You know my uncle gave me the nickname 'Boy'. I actually hate it, but it has stuck with me ever since. If we are going to do business together, you must call me by my real name."

"And what would that be?" Danny asked.

"Eduardo."

JEEPNEYS ARE RELICS of the WWII-era military jeep with the back extended. There is also a different version for private citizens and non-commercial use with the chassis in the original short version. The "family" jeeps were called *owners*.

"Hop in," Eduardo said, jumping into the driver side of his stainless steel owner.

Eduardo sped along the main avenue, his eyes fixed on the traffic ahead trying to avoid a collision with the vehicles abruptly changing lanes. The wind blowing in Danny and Helen's faces felt good as it dried the sweat on their foreheads from the humid night. Their owner passed by vendors on the side street frying plantain bananas and yams covered in brown sugar. Several carts with propane-powered, portable stoves were selling fried fish balls on a large wok filled with hot oil.

"It's very important that we don't tell anyone about what we're doing," Danny said.

"I'll try. Why are you worried about that?" Eduardo asked.

"Without getting into too much detail, someone is after the compound that I need to bring to Commander Berto in exchange for my friend," Danny said.

"The problem with this business is that it's hard to trust the people selling the information to locate Commander Berto," Eduardo said.

"What do you mean?" Helen asked.

"As soon as the word is out that we're trying to make contact with him, we never really know who had also paid them in order to get to you. For the right price, everyone is willing to sell just about anything. The meeting place could be a decoy, and once we're there we could be ambushed. But don't worry, I know exactly what to do. I will go ahead of you and scout the location myself, and if I smell anything fishy I will text or call you right away to abort," Eduardo said.

"How will you make contact with Commander Berto if the Armed Forces of the Philippines themselves couldn't locate him?" Helen asked.

"I know people. Where do you think these people buy their guns but through intermediaries like me. I have to make a few calls as soon as I get back to the club. Where are you staying?"

EDUARDO PARKED THE OWNER in front of the hotel where Danny and Helen were staying for the night. Danny shifted his gaze at the tourists walking in the main entrance with shopping bags and swimwear.

"The money?" Eduardo said, turning to Danny.

Helen unzipped her backpack and placed a stack of hundred-dollar bills on his hand.

"That's five grand," Danny said.

"This won't even cover the cell phone minutes I'll spend calling people."

"The money we have is limited," Helen said. "We still

have to pay Commander Berto a million bucks."

Not wanting to get into an argument over money and worried that Eduardo might decide to back out, Danny placed another stack of bills on his lap. "That's ten grand altogether now. You can buy lots of fighting cocks with that."

"I like you two already."

"I will personally give you another five grand as a bonus when we get Blake back alive and safely back to Manila," Helen added.

Eduardo inspected the stack of money and thumbed through it. He placed it under his nose and sniffed it.

"I love the smell of American money. Benjamin Franklin couldn't be more handsome," he said as he pocketed the money, grinning.

"How do we know that you're not going to bail out?" Danny asked.

"Relax. You two are too tense. I'll get things rolling here. You know where I live. Besides, I want the additional five grand as a bonus, rewarding me for my hard work once we get your friend back nice and safe," Eduardo said, winking. "Now I have to go to work and look for some bad guys. Once I start calling and paying people off, things will happen real fast. Stay by your phone."

A GIFT BASKET FILLED with *pili nuts, pastillas, ensaymada* and packages of dried mangoes was sitting on top of the table when they walked into their room. Helen laid down on the bed under the thin, white canopy cascading off the ceiling like a waterfall.

Danny slid next to her. "When this whole thing is over, are you going back to Boston right away?"

"The school year is ending soon and I have some tidying up to do."

Danny laid on his side, resting his cheek on his hand. "I'd be very happy if you move in with me."

From the expression on her face, Danny sensed that Helen was intrigued by his question. She said nothing and just stared at the overhead canopy. The situation became awkward, as if they were teenagers contemplating if they should be a steady couple. A minute later, she broke the silence.

"Do you think it's a good idea?"

"No matter what happens when we return to San Diego—with or without Blake—I want you back in my life."

"What makes you think it's going to work this time?"

"I can't be a bachelor forever and I need you in my life."

"What are you saying?" Helen responded while running her fingers in his hair.

Danny dug inside his backpack sitting on the floor and retrieved a small cloth bag with a pearl ring inside. Helen sat up on the bed, curious what he was doing.

He knelt in front of her and held up the pearl ring.

"Will you marry me?"

Danny watched her eyes as they focused on the

glistening pearl resting atop its shiny silver band. She appeared as if she was trying to process his simple question. Danny knew that she loved him too, and from the hints she had been suggesting during their past week together, she didn't want to be alone in her cold and empty Boston apartment.

"Yes, Danny, I would be very happy to marry you," she replied, kissing him on the lips.

Danny took her left hand and placed the ring on her finger.

"I promise to love you forever," Danny said.

Danny could count the few times he was truly happy in his life—Helen agreeing to be his wife ranked on top.

Danny climbed into bed and tenderly pulled Helen down next to him, staring at his future wife. He planted a long, lingering kiss on her pink lips. He kissed the top of her shoulders and ran his tongue across each of her earlobes. Helen let out a sigh of pleasure. With his left hand, he reached for the lampshade on the nightstand and flicked it off.

THE CELL PHONE woke Danny up. He lifted Helen's arm off of his chest and gently pushed her leg off of his thigh. Helen rolled away from him. The morning sun highlighted the smooth skin on her naked back. For the first time since they broke up, Danny and Helen made love, twice in one night. The first time was before going to bed and the second was when Danny woke up in the middle of the night to Helen's tender kisses.

He looked at the screen and recognized Eduardo's number. There was a kind of hurry in the way the phone rang, as if it wanted to be picked up right away. He imagined what Eduardo would tell him—either the bad news that Commander Berto had stayed quiet in his hideout and couldn't be located, or to pack up and get ready to leave right away to meet him.

"Eduardo?"

"Danny, it's your lucky day. I'm in Zamboanga City right now. I flew out last night a few hours after we talked," Eduardo replied.

"Were you able to contact Commander Berto?" Danny said as he nervously anticipated what Eduardo was going to tell him.

"Not just that. I was able to set up a meeting with him this afternoon. You need to get the money and the Cube and fly it out here as soon as possible. Commander Berto wants to meet at a secret location in the city."

"I need to drive back to Manila to get the Cube. It's stored in a deposit box. As soon as we get it, we'll fly there right away."

"Great. Text me before you leave. I need to meet you at the airport."

DANNY SHUT THE PHONE. His ordeal was getting closer to being resolved. Blake was finally coming home and the thought of it lifted his spirit. He dialed

Melchor's number, eager to share the latest development.

"We finally got a hold of Commander Berto and he wants us to meet him in Zamboanga City," Danny said.

"That's great news. I left the hospital to be safe. I think the damn driver I hired was feeding information to Dr. Klein."

"How do you know?"

"He keeps asking questions about where we're going next. I began to suspect something wasn't right."

"Where are you now?"

"I'm hiding out in a friend's house. Hire a van to take you here, then we'll go to the airport together and fly out right away," Melchor said.

DR. KLEIN WAS SITTING at a table in a beerhouse watching a drunken man singing karaoke when his phone rang.

"I just received orders to fly them."

"When and where?"

"I was only told to be on standby and to be ready to fly within a moment's notice. It could be anywhere," the pilot said.

"Very well," Dr. Klein said. "I will compensate you for your information. See how easy it is to do business with me? I'm in Baguio City right now looking for Danny and his girlfriend. Bastards got away from me again."

"I will contact you as soon as I know."

Dr. Klein swallowed a mouthful of beer and looked out

the window. He knew that by the end of the day, the Cube would be his.

Fourteen

THE WHITE VAN ARRIVED in front of the hotel an hour later. Danny felt both trepidation and excitement knowing he would either come back home with Blake unharmed or their meeting would be another bust. The thought of Dr. Klein intercepting them again came to mind, but since their rendezvous was kept a secret he was confident that things would go well.

The driver negotiated his way through the sluggish traffic of yellow Jeepneys and owners along Magsaysay Drive. Danny noticed the Paradise East club with doors wide open as it aired out the stink of cigarette smoke and the smell of human odors that had occupied it all night.

It was Good Friday and Olongapo City felt desolate. The streets were absent of the usual hubbub of activities— no patrons going in the restaurants, no shoppers with bags of goodies walking out of stores, and no kids in their school uniforms running along the sidewalks.

As they exited the city, they passed by the rotunda—the bust of the *"apo"* stood erect. According to legends, the apo, or wise leader, who tried dearly to get the warring tribes to stop fighting each other was decapitated and his head was placed on a bamboo pole. The people called out *"olo ng apo,"* or "head of the wise leader." The word became part of the tribe's vocabulary and eventually morphed into the word Olongapo, for which the city was named.

The buses coming out of the terminal followed the van. Danny looked back at the bust getting smaller as they moved farther away from the city. He thought of their meeting with Commander Berto and hoped that Blake would not meet the same gruesome ending as the apo.

AS THEY were approaching the municipality of Dinalupihan in the province of Bataan, they encountered slow traffic. They rolled the windows down, curious what was going on. Bystanders were gathered on the side of the road watching a man in a red robe carry a black cross on his shoulder, re-enacting Jesus on his way to the Calvary on the day he was crucified. The man playing the part of Jesus struggled as he stepped forward, slowly dragging the cross on the hot cement street.

A row of shirtless men with red cloths covering their faces appeared around the bend, self-flagellating their backs with the slivers of bamboo bound to their ropes.

Bright red blood was smeared all over their backs, dripping down their white pants. Their relentless beating had peeled off their skin's top layer.

"What are they doing to themselves?" Helen asked as horror resonated in her voice.

"It's called *penitensya,* or penance. These men are trying to punish themselves for all the bad deeds they've committed throughout the year," Danny answered.

"Isn't that practice discouraged by the church?" Helen asked.

"I don't think the practice will ever be stopped. It has been going on for generations. Men vowed to do this because of a favor they had prayed for. Some of the men have loved ones who are very sick, and some of them are in very tough situations. By doing the penitensya, they are hoping that their worries will be solved."

A group of men performing the ritual stopped at a station where women were chanting a prayer. The men lay on their stomachs and spread their arms in the shape of the cross. A group of men with flat wooden sticks, began whacking their buttocks.

"My God!" Helen said, flinching.

Danny buried her face in his chest to shield her from the self-deprecating act. Danny thought of the bargain he made with God when he was at the San Agustin church. He wondered if it was good enough to get Blake back. Maybe he needed to make a promise and do the penitensya.

As soon as they found a sliver of space in the crowd, they carefully maneuvered for the town's exit.

DANNY FELT RIGHT AT HOME when they finally arrived in Metro Manila, its familiar streets choked with Jeepneys belching smoke, stopped in the middle of the road to take more passengers. Thousands of commuters stood patiently on the side of the road waiting for a ride that would either take them to work or back home.

The view of the Andres Bonifacio Monument looked intimidating from afar. The beige obelisk towering over the city of Caloocan reminded everyone passing by of the bloody history of the country and the sacrifices that the people made to win their freedom from Spanish rule. Andres Bonifacio stood proudly in front of the flag and the revolutionaries holding up bolos, shouting battle cries to their brethren.

MELCHOR WAS SITTING on a chair drinking a cup of coffee when Danny and Helen arrived.

"Just in time," Melchor said.

"Are you sure you're okay? You don't have to come with us," Helen said.

"What are you saying? I'm not afraid of Commander Berto. Especially now that I know his men are lousy shooters. I want to be there when Blake is released."

"Then I guess we can go now," Danny said.

THE VAN WAS ROUNDING the corner when the cars in front began to slow down. A greasy-haired, political candidate wearing a red, white and blue vest was standing on the flatbed truck with a picture of his face and his name on large banners. His promises were written in big bold letters for the world to see, passing by with his convoy of supporters trailing behind. He waved at the crowd along the way, all expecting to catch a freebie of T-shirts and hats tossed from the truck.

"These politicians! Some of them never do anything good for the nation," Melchor said. "Turn down that street. We must get out of here fast or we're going to be late."

While the van was driving through a narrow street just wide enough for a large truck to get through, the noise from the candidate's megaphone and the shouts from the throng of people faded in the distance. Four blocks later, the staccato sound of a police siren suddenly began to wail. Danny looked behind him and saw police lights flashing.

"What a pest," Melchor remarked.

A policeman approached the car, adjusting his baseball cap.

"What's going on?" Helen asked.

"Some sort of traffic violation," Danny said, worried at the impending delay.

"What seems to be the problem, officer?" Melchor asked.

"This is a one-way street. You didn't see the sign?" the officer said with intimidating eyes. "Your license, please."

While the officer read the information on the card, Melchor tried to neutralize the situation. "I'm really sorry. We're new in this area. I'm taking my friends to the airport and we're running late. With your kindness, sir, can I just leave the fine with you? They can't miss their flight back to America."

The policeman pretended to write something on his ticket book and said nothing. It felt like an eternity for each minute that the policeman dragged out the situation. Though Melchor knew it was illegal to bribe public officials, not everyone was honest and he knew how the game was played.

"I'm doing you a favor today. I don't normally do this," the policeman said, giving the license back to the driver. "See that kid in the corner selling gum and cigarettes? Buy a pack of cigarettes and pay him five hundred pesos. Then you're free to go."

FINALLY GAINING SPEED, they reached Epifanio de los Santos Avenue. It was the site of the People Power Revolution—the extraordinary moment in Philippine history in February 1986 when hundreds of thousands of people flooded the streets of Manila wanting the current regime out. Nuns equipped only with rosaries, priests wielding wooden crosses, students holding banners, and housewives carrying the statue of the Virgin

Mary begged the military armed to the teeth not to fire on the innocent civilians. Young women offered flowers to the battle-weary soldiers. Both men and boys pushed tanks with their bare hands, as if they could stop the behemoth from advancing and crushing them.

Then suddenly, as if by deus ex machina, helicopters sent by the United States appeared in the sky. Twenty-plus years of a leader that would seem to go on for another decade were finally over.

"BACK SO QUICKLY?" the bank manager asked.

"Can you help us get our things?" Helen asked.

"Sure...come this way," the manager said, ushering them to the bank vault.

The bank manager inserted his key in the slot and unlocked the boxes. With their personal keys, Danny and Helen unlocked the safety deposit boxes and transferred the Cube to their rollaway luggage.

"We need to close our account. We won't be needing the safety deposit boxes anymore," Helen said, handing her key to the bank manager.

"You may keep it as a souvenir. We'll be replacing the lock as soon as you leave."

Danny pocketed the key and hoped that he'd never have to use it ever again.

WITH A TENSE LOOK in his face, the pilot stood by the wing of the chartered airplane and waited for instructions from Melchor on where to go.

"We're going to Zamboanga City," Melchor said, climbing into the cabin.

The pilot nodded and sauntered around the plane's tail section pretending to do a preflight inspection. When no one was looking, he texted their flight information to Dr. Klein.

Fifteen

THE DARK BROWN SUV was already waiting outside the airport when Danny, Helen and Melchor arrived. The air was thick with humidity and the ground was hot from the early afternoon April sun. Danny could feel his shirt sticking to his back.

"Commander Berto and his men are waiting for us in a warehouse outside of the city to make the electronic transfer and to receive the Cube," Eduardo said from the driver's seat.

ZAMBOANGA—the largest city built on the southern part of Mindanao Island where its centuries-old problems coexist with its present-day headaches. The SUV moved freely through streets that were just as crowded as Manila. Men on motorcycles squeezed through tight spaces between vehicles, barely wide enough for the width of their handlebars to fit through.

They were all silent in the back of the SUV not knowing where Eduardo was taking them. A layer of worry gripped Danny as he thought of how the day would turn out. The meeting seemed like the same old song and dance they had previously done. They were driving around the city as if they were a group of tourists on a chartered bus. He looked out the window and saw a white mosque with a red dome and red-tipped minarets out in the distance. In the back of his mind, Danny wanted to protest to get things going but he knew that Eduardo was in charge of the situation and there wasn't a thing he could do.

They just had passed by the old Fort Pilar, a defense bastion against looming pirates from the nearby islands, built by the Spaniards in the 1600s, when out of frustration Helen asked, "Why are we wasting time and not going directly to Blake?"

"We need to keep driving around until I'm sure that Dr. Klein or the military is not following us. We don't need any surprises. We're almost there," Eduardo replied.

The SUV traced the road along the bay. People were sitting on the concrete seawall and enjoying the ocean breeze. Container and passenger ships floated in the distance. Women in long blouses and headscarves walked lazily along the water. The *vinta*—boats with colorful striped patterns of red and blue sails—floated near the shore.

"Basilan Island is about ten miles that way," Eduardo

said, pointing out to sea. "Commander Berto's main hideout is in those mountains."

"Is that where those men have been keeping Blake?" Danny asked.

It was strange that Basilan Island was only a stone's throw from a modern city like Zamboanga, yet no one could rescue him—even with the military's entire arsenal of boats, helicopters and armored personnel-carriers.

About half an hour later when Eduardo was confident that no one was following them, he decided that the time was right to meet with Kulog ng Timog.

THE SUV STOPPED in front of a warehouse with corrugated tin walls surrounded by old tires collecting dust, stacked around the building.

"Let's go. They're waiting for us," Eduardo said, getting out of the vehicle.

They followed him to a closed door on the side of the building. The place was eerily quiet and it seemed like no one was inside. Eduardo dialed a number on his phone. Danny heard him start talking in Chavacano—a Spanish-based dialect spoken in the area.

"I'm glad you're able to speak Chavacano," Danny said.

"I grew up around here. That's why some of these bandits trust me, thinking I'm one of their own," Eduardo replied.

When the side door finally opened, a man in black pants with an AK-47 hanging from his shoulder greeted them with a straight face. They followed the man to the warehouse, walking straight into the belly of the beast and not knowing what to expect when they finally met with Blake.

Commander Berto and his men were sitting around the table with their rifles resting on their laps, playing cards and eating *halo-halo* (shaved ice with evaporated milk), sweet beans, coconut, and toasted rice topped with purple ice cream. Danny found it odd that the mood in the room was so calm, as if it was just another day at office.

"Did you enjoy the tour of the city? Because I hate surprises popping out of the bushes," Commander Berto asked.

"Where's Blake?" Helen asked.

"Relax…I haven't cut his head off. At least not yet. We treat our paying guests here, especially foreigners with such out-of-this-world island hospitality."

"Please…where's Blake?" Danny asked.

Commander Berto snapped his fingers. A henchman with a pistol tucked into his belt dragged out Blake. Although Blake walked on his own power, he looked weak from the captivity that had been going on for more than two weeks.

"Are you okay?" Helen asked, rushing into his arms and hugging him tight.

"Just a bit dehydrated from the heat but I'm fine," Blake responded.

"Enough of that drama. You'll all be together soon

enjoying the California sunshine as soon as you give me the money and the Cube," Commander Berto said squeezing himself between Helen and Blake—separating them. "As soon as we get things going here, the sooner we're all going home in time for dinner. Where's your little gadget?"

Helen pulled out the touchpad and inserted the cable into the laptop's USB port. She entered her account number and password into the bank's website. Commander Berto handed her a piece of paper with his account number written on it. Helen keyed in the information and placed her thumb on the scanner. A few seconds later, her thumbprints were verified and a green check mark next to her name flashed on the screen. Commander Berto escorted Blake to the computer. He placed his thumb on the scanner. After his biometrics were validated, a box with the text "Transfer Now" began to blink. Below it, the amount of $900,000.00 was displayed. With the computer's touchpad, Helen completed the transfer.

"There you go. You got your million dollars. Here's the Cube," Danny said, thrusting the rollaway to Commander Berto. "Can we go home now with Blake?"

"You're not off the hook yet, cowboy. I have boats waiting for us on the beach to take us back to Basilan Island. I don't want a repeat performance of what had happened to us back in Tawi-Tawi. Once we're on the boat, we will let you go," Commander Berto said. "I need you as insurance just in case the military is waiting for an ambush. Then you'll never see me again."

"How can we be sure that you'll release us when we get to the beach?" Danny asked.

"Looks like you have no choice, huh?" Commander Berto said, pointing his AK-47 at Danny. "You two get in the van with me and Blake. That's not a request."

With no other choice but to comply, they climbed into the van.

"What about us?" Melchor asked.

"You and Eduardo stay in the SUV you came with and follow us closely."

NOBODY WAS TALKING IN THE VAN—the only sound Danny could hear was the pinging sound of the diesel engine puttering along the asphalt road. Danny stole a glance at Commander Berto who was checking and rechecking the magazine clips around his waist. If he had a nonchalant way of conducting his business earlier, this time Danny could see the tension in his movements.

As they were speeding along a curve in the road, a man in a straw hat towing a carabao suddenly appeared in front of them. The driver slammed on the brakes. The animal bowed its head down, pointing its long, crescent-shaped horns at the van.

"Get moving, old man!" Commander Berto shouted.

The man in the straw hat pulled the rope attached to a metal ring on the carabao's nose, but the animal didn't want to take a step forward. Impatient, Commander Berto pulled out his pistol and fired several shots in the air. The screams of gunfire ricocheted inside the van. Danny and Helen winced at the noise. Danny heard Commander Berto order the driver to go around the carabao. The driver stepped on the gas and they continued moving along the two-lane concrete road.

As the van was getting near the beach, coconut trees began to appear in the distance, swaying freely in the afternoon breeze. They were less than a football field away from the waiting speedboats.

Straight up ahead, three oncoming vehicles were approaching them at high speeds as if determined to hit them head on. The driver quickly reacted by jerking the steering wheel to the right to avoid being hit, but his hasty action caused the van to swerve to the shoulder. The tires got stuck in the soft soil and the van couldn't move forward.

"Get out! Get out!" Commander Berto shouted. "We need to run to the beach."

Danny felt a strong grip on his arm pulling him out. The armed men were pushing Blake and Helen out, too. Danny grabbed the rollaway containing the Cube to save it from getting lost in the confusion. As soon as he was out in the open, he turned his attention to the group of cars. To his dismay, he saw Dr. Klein getting out of the van with a pistol in his hand, surrounded by several men with assault rifles.

Bullets began popping from every direction. Danny saw the man who brought out Blake earlier at the warehouse fall to the ground, thick blood oozing from his chest and neck.

Danny immediately draped his arms around Helen's shoulders, pulled her down to the ground, and shielded her with his body. He covered his ears to muffle the sounds of the gunfire erupting all around him. The barrage of bullets from all directions was nonstop. Danny surveyed his immediate surroundings to get away from the line of fire. Seeing a large rock bulging from the ground several yards away, he signaled Helen to crawl slowly behind it. As he crouched next to the rock, trying dearly not to get hit by the onslaught of bullets, it was all he could do to survive the chaos swirling around him and to try to stay alive until the afternoon bloodbath was over.

There was a sudden lull from the shooting as Dr. Klein and his men reloaded their weapons. Finding an opportunity to flee, Commander Berto jumped at Danny and Helen, pulled them up by their shoulders, and shouted, "Get moving and run to the beach!"

Two of Commander Berto's men stayed behind and sprayed bullets in order to stop Dr. Klein and his men from advancing.

Danny tried to hurry, but the added weight of dragging the Cube through the softening soil beneath his feet made it difficult. Pushed by Kulog ng Timog, Blake and Helen tried as fast as they could to keep up. All Danny could think of was getting to the beach where the speedboats were waiting to hand off the Cube to Commander Berto. It was the only way to set themselves free and to get Dr. Klein off his back.

Just as Danny snuck a peak behind him to see where Dr. Klein and his men were, he heard a series of *rat-tat-tat* sounds. Danny, Helen and Blake hit the ground fast. Dr. Klein and his mercenaries were coming after them with a relentless barrage of bullets. Commander Berto and his men answered back by unleashing hell with their AK-47 assault rifles and grenade launchers to keep them back.

A projectile exploded as soon as it hit the sand several yards from Danny and Helen. A flash of bright yellow phosphorous light blinded Danny. The nearby plants split open from the impact. The explosion sounded different. It was like a father's booming voice telling his kids to stop fighting. Danny searched the immediate area where the grenade was launched. When his eyes finally adjusted from the explosion and back to the golden hue of the afternoon light, he saw two military trucks stopped in the middle of the street. Half of the soldiers were jumping out of the truck bed while the other half fired indiscriminately at anything that moved.

From his vantage point, Danny could see the speedboats waiting at the beach, facing out toward the ocean with engines idling. Danny thought of telling Helen and Blake to run to the soldiers for their safety but quickly realized that Commander Berto wouldn't hesitate to put a bullet in their backs. Fearing for their lives, he held his tongue.

THE SITUATION was quickly becoming a lopsided fight. Commander Berto and his men shot back at the government troops to keep their distance, but were no match against the well-equipped and well-trained Scout Rangers. Out of sheer desperation, Commander Berto grabbed Helen and pointed his Colt 45 pistol to her head.

"No! Please don't do that! Take the goddamn compound and let her go!" Danny screamed through the gunfire around him.

"Throw me the compound!" Commander Berto shouted back.

Danny picked up the rollaway. Just as he was about to hurl it at Commander Berto, a stinging sensation pulsed through his left leg and he felt his pants get moist. Helen's eyes widened. He prodded around the area where the pain was coming from to find bright red blood oozing out his left calf. Almost immediately, another bullet wheezed by his head and hit Commander Berto directly in his left shoulder.

"Fucking shit!" Commander Berto shouted in pain, loosening his vise-like grip on Helen's arm. Helen quickly pushed him away and dove behind a fallen tree. Danny spotted a wooden stick lying on the ground, picked it up, and in a single fluid motion slammed it into Commander Berto's injured shoulder. The Commander grimaced in pain, dropping the Colt 45. He followed up with another blow to Commander Berto's right wrist and then thrusted the stick into his stomach. Although Danny feared Commander Berto's wrath, he was more terrified by the Scout Rangers' indiscriminate machine gun fire. As Commander Berto fell to the ground, Danny dashed over to Helen, lying flat on the ground to avoid getting hit in the crossfire.

"Where's Blake?" Helen asked.

"I can't see him."

"How's your leg?" Helen asked.

"The bullet just grazed my calf. It hurts like hell but I'm okay."

FROM THE PROTECTION of several fallen coconut trees, Danny scanned the surroundings and saw Dr. Klein and Commander Berto standing over the Cube.

"What the fuck are you trying to do? I hired you to do a job and now you think you're taking over?" Dr. Klein said. His face seethed with anger.

"I don't need the petty half-million dollars you're paying me. I can sell the compound directly to the fishing company and make five times more. Why don't you move aside, old man, before I blow your brains out," Commander Berto laughed.

"You fucking low life scum. Just because a heron is standing on the back of the carabao doesn't make it mightier. You're just a common criminal for hire and now you think you're above the people who pay you?"

Dr. Klein kicked Commander Berto in the stomach and grabbed the rollaway. As he stepped forward, Commander Berto grabbed him by the waist and threw him to the ground. Klein spun around and landed a hard blow on Commander Berto's injured left shoulder. Stunned by the pain, Commander Berto released him.

Carrying the rollaway over his head, Dr. Klein began running as fast as he could away from Commander Berto, headed toward the safety of the advancing soldiers.

Commander Berto got up quickly and ran after him. Inches behind Dr. Klein, he jumped him. Both of them fell down. He yanked the rollaway from Klein. Not wanting to give up easily, Klein threw several hard punches into his face and chest and thrust his head into Commander Berto's stomach. They exchanged punches while rolling around the ground. With brute force, Commander Berto maneuvered on top of Dr. Klein and delivered several hard blows to his forehead and jaw, knocking him out.

Commander Berto was about to retrieve the rollaway and run towards the waiting boats when gunfire suddenly erupted from the soldiers' direction. Aware that the firepower the Scout Rangers were unleashing could eventually finish him, he ducked to avoid getting shot at. Clumps of sand exploded around him.

The shooting stopped a few minutes later. Someone on the megaphone from the military's direction announced, "Raise your hands above your head and slowly get up or we will start shooting again until you are all dead. This is your last chance."

Commander Berto turned toward Dr. Klein who was slowly getting up. He reached down for the handgun strapped to his ankle, carefully walked behind Klein, and pushed the gun's muzzle against the back of his head.

"Don't make a move, or you're dead!"

"You're surrounded. Why don't you just give up?" Dr. Klein said.

"Shut up, old man. If I die, you die, too. Now get up and tell the Ranger boys to stop shooting or you will meet your maker by sunset."

Dr. Klein slowly rose, waving his arms at the troops.

"Cease fire!"

The soldiers approached from all directions with their M-16s aimed at Commander Berto and his men.

"Back off or this Yankee is dead!" Commander Berto shouted.

The Scout Ranger platoon leader ordered his men to stand down. The soldiers immediately pointed their weapons up in the air. Commander Berto wrapped his arm around Dr. Klein's neck and towed him back to the beach. The soldiers were powerless to do anything. All they could do was watch as Commander Berto and his band of thugs left with yet another hostage.

Commander Berto pushed Dr. Klein onto the speedboat and jumped in. The sounds of the revving motors thundered—disturbing the blood-orange afternoon sky. They pointed their speedboats into the vast cloak of the open sea. Then, just like a dream, the group who kidnapped Blake disappeared into the setting sun— taking the same man who hired them to do the dirty deeds.

THE ENTIRE FIELD became quiet. Danny and Helen slowly rose from behind the fallen tree trunk, searching for Blake's whereabouts. To their astonishment, five Scout Rangers with their M-16s were standing in front of them.

"Sergeant...we were taken by Commander Berto," Danny said.

The soldiers lowered their weapons.

"Aren't you going after Commander Berto?" Helen asked.

"We'll get him," the platoon leader replied. "Their boats aren't too far. We already radioed for assistance and the Navy patrol boats are already in pursuit as we speak."

"Thank you for rescuing us," Helen added.

"We're sorry to tell you, but we believe that Kulog ng Timog has taken Blake Mason with them," the platoon leader said.

"I'm over here!"

Blake stood waving his arms from across the field.

Danny and Helen ran to Blake ecstatic that he was unharmed and wrapped their arms around him. The three of them hugged each other very tight while tears of joy rolled down their cheeks. The outcome of the afternoon couldn't have been more perfect. They were all together and free at last.

"We're all alive," Blake said jubilantly.

The soldiers slung their rifles on their shoulders and returned in single file to the transport truck without a hint of urgency on their footsteps.

Danny looked up at the fading afternoon sky as the coconut tree leaves rustled in the wind. Like a revelation, it came to him. Blake wasn't the first person kidnapped in Mindanao and probably wouldn't be the last. Something had to be done to stop a crisis like this from happening again, but he didn't know where to start.

From a distance, Danny saw the Cube neglected in the sand. For the past two weeks, it was at the center of Blake's misery. Now, no one wanted to claim it.

"Let's get out of here," Danny said as he put his arms around his best friend and the woman he loved.

Epilogue

THE SUN SHONE BRIGHTLY against his face. The waves were crashing on the shore at La Jolla Cove. Danny stood next to Blake and looked at the sea of guests sitting in the white folding chairs embellished with flowers. Five months after Danny and Helen returned from the Philippines, Helen accepted a teaching position in San Diego. And they finally decided to tie the knot.

"Jeff just told me earlier that we've received a large donation from a certain rich somebody. He wouldn't say who is funding our research, and this time it will be a complete secret with a dedicated research vessel," Danny said.

"Where are we going next?" Blake asked, turning to Danny at the white arbor.

"I heard the best place to conduct our research is off the coast of eastern Africa."

"You gotta be kidding me."

"Relax. Now that I already know what to do, Alaska is the farthest place we will go. We can even go fly fishing while we're up there."

"Good," Blake remarked with relief in his voice. "I'd like to be home for dinner after each day of hard work."

"Do you think she's coming? She's not going to be a runaway bride, is she?"

"Chillax…Helen planned this for months and paid for the wedding herself. I don't think she's going to do that," Blake remarked with a smile.

"That's something I will never understand. How come the woman pays for the wedding?"

"That's why I'm not marrying a Filipina. I don't want to pay for the wedding," Blake said in a friendly banter.

"No matter what you decide, you'll eventually surrender your paycheck to your future wife…wherever she's from. That's the tradition worldwide."

Danny looked down at his wristwatch. The wedding was supposed to start at five p.m., but fifteen minutes had already gone by.

"She's not your wife yet, but she's already on Filipino time," Blake said with a grin.

THE WEDDING PROCESSION BEGAN. Melchor and his wife walked slowly down the aisle with their arms locked together. Danny was glad that he had accepted his invitation to be his godfather. Traditionally, that meant that from now on Melchor would help Danny with all his affairs in life. He smiled at Danny before sitting in the front row. The entourage followed.

Helen got out of the limousine. Danny squinted his eyes to see how she looked. She was wearing a white, sleeveless wedding gown with a transparent veil trailing behind her. The quartet played the wedding march. Six months ago, Danny would have never thought that such a wonderful day would ever come. But there she was at the end of the aisle, ready to meet him at the altar. The guests stood up. Slowly, Helen sauntered towards where Danny was waiting, sprinkling her warm smile at the guests snapping photos.

Helen hooked her arm around Danny and the two of them faced the priest.

The candle sponsors lit the candles. The veil sponsors pinned the thin white veil onto their formal wear. The cord sponsors placed a figure-eight cord over their shoulders.

Danny brought his lips to Helen's ear.

"Looks like we're stuck together for life," he whispered.

"I think that's the plan," Helen said, laughing under her breath at his comment.

After the priest pronounced them "husband and wife", they faced each other. Danny stared into Helen's blue-grey eyes for a brief moment. Ever so slowly, he kissed her on the lips, elated to have finally kissed her for the first time as his wife.

THEY STROLLED TO THE GUESTS gathered around a white, bell-shaped box hanging on a wrought iron arch by the cliff. Simultaneously, they pulled the white ribbons hanging on the bottom. The bell split open and hundreds of butterflies flew out into the cool San Diego sky.